Signs of Martha

SIGNS

of

MARTHA

Sarah Raymond

GREAT PLAINS
TEEN FICTION

Great Plains Teen Fiction
(an imprint of Great Plains Publications)
345-955 Portage Avenue
Winnipeg, MB R3G 0P9
www.greatplains.mb.ca

Great Plains Publications gratefully acknowledges the financial support provided for its publishing program by the Government of Canada through the Canada Book Fund; the Canada Council for the Arts; the Province of Manitoba through the Book Publishing Tax Credit and the Book Publisher Marketing Assistance Program; and the Manitoba Arts Council.

TORONTO ARTS COUNCIL The Author wishes to acknowledge the support of the City of Toronto through the Toronto Arts Council

Design & Typography by Relish Design Studio Ltd.
Printed in Canada by Friesens

"Our House, the Tourist Attraction", a Martha short story, was first published in *The Antigonish Review* in 2008.

LIBRARY AND ARCHIVES CANADA CATALOGUING IN PUBLICATION

Raymond, Sarah
  Signs of Martha / Sarah Raymond.

ISBN 978-1-926531-09-0
I. Title.

PS8639.A955S54 2011   jC813'.6   C2010-907111-5

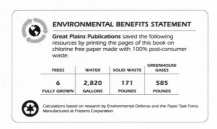

Many thanks to Susie Berg, Pat Bourke, Sarah Byck,
Karen Krossing, Shari Lapena, Patricia McCowan
and Karen Rankin for their support and encouragement;
to Peter Carver, Barbara Greenwood, Sharon Jennings
and Kim Moritsugu for their generous instruction;
to Anita Daher for editorial help; and to Sam, Mitsuko
and especially Vince for sticking with me along
the bumpy road to writing a first novel.

Chapter 1

THREE WOBBLY ROWS OF PLANTS edge the alfalfa field in the Schellenbergers' back acreage. Bernie is picking cukes a half a dozen fence posts ahead of me with her arse poking in the air. She reminds me of one of those wooden cut-outs of a cartoon gardener with her frilly underwear showing. Bernie and I have been growing cucumbers for more summers than I care to count, but at age sixteen, I figure I can endure one last season. At least Lowe's Pickles pays up nice—as long as we don't let our vegetables swell into fat middle-aged things, soft in the middle.

I push hair off my forehead but it falls back where it came from. I have assorted, sun-bleached layers that are congested with split ends and generally neglected. Too much time dreaming, I guess. Not enough self-maintenance. I lift a vine sagging with cucumbers, strip it and let it drop on the dirt. Prod it a little and then *voila*. The vine draws the contour of a heart. "Bernie," I yell up at her. "Check this out."

A fountain of cucumbers arcs over her head and sprays into the bushel basket. "Another garter snake?" she calls back. As per usual, Bernie can't sacrifice a moment of picking.

"Better. A vision of thigh-quivering lust and desire!"

Bernie tosses a doubtful glance backwards. "Let's have a look then." She traipses back, squats and peers down past her major schnoz. Bernie has suffered the odd remark because of her nose, but I think it's proud looking. Maybe she sees her dad's hooked variety when she looks in the mirror. You could hang a cup off that one.

I point to the curled vine. "It's a heart, Bern."

Bernie's eyebrows knot up. Poor kid. She's not an expert in the field of art or love. "That's all?"

"What do you mean 'that's all?' Don't you see? Passion can grow in the most unlikely places." Bern, two years older than me, has never had a boyfriend. Try meeting guys when you're a year outside school, at home collecting eggs and picking cukes. She's been saving up for college. Nutrition or something. At least she's got that road all paved for herself.

"In a cucumber patch?" Bernie peers across the field to the sun, launching its journey up the sky. "Anyway, let's get back to work."

"Aw, Bern. I'll die of boredom. Stay here and pick with me."

I know Bernie would rather finish her row than help pick mine, but to keep me happy, she bends over and lifts a vine.

I hunker low and yank off a cuke. "How about that guy with the AC/DC shirt at the grading station? He was looking at you." Well, he was looking *near* her, at the load of cucumbers she dumped onto the conveyor belt, but Bernie needs encouragement.

She shudders and wags "No thank you" with an overgrown cucumber.

"Too sweaty?"

"Too skinny." Bernie has a sturdy build herself. She's shaped like a brick almost, not that I'd mention it, although our friend Leanne has.

I get an idea. "Then tell me. If we had one of those flatbed trailers for picking that you drag behind a tractor—"

"The kind you lie down on?" She shoots the cuke into my basket.

"On your stomach. Yeah. Who would you lie down and pick with? Could be anyone in the world. Famous or regular. Rippled or ketchup flavoured."

"I don't know, Martha." Bernie elbows a mosquito away. She's an awesome picker, but when it comes to imagination games, you need a team of draft horses to drag the ideas out.

"Then what kind of person would you choose? Somebody funny and sweet who shares his Chiclets and remembers how you're ticklish behind the knees?"

"But I'm not ticklish behind—"

"But just imagine." I lean upright. Personally, I have a boyfriend. I'm just trying to help out ol' Bern. "Or would you go for someone more mysterious? Who smokes roll-your-owns? Maybe tobacco, maybe not. And hangs around the plaza, leaning against the wall." I step carefully over our row and saunter to the fencepost. Fold my arms across my chest and fake a long drag on a cuke. "Like this, Bernie."

I get a titter out of her. "He doesn't say much," I go on, "but when he looks at you with those brown eyes lurking behind his thickets of lashes, he tunnels straight into your soul. Even into the nasty, shadowy bits around the edges. Only he doesn't mind those bits. They only make him want you more." Under the spell of the imaginary guy, my grip on the vegetable softens.

Bernie stops picking to consider and says, "I wouldn't care for either of those types." She darts her eyes left and right, like she's on the lookout for garden spies. "Don't tell anyone else, Martha Becker."

"I'd never, Bern. I swear." I figure she means Tammy Mills and Leanne. I return to the row, straddle the plants and squat low.

"I'd share a flatbed with..." Bernie itches her nose with her flowered garden glove.

"Who?"

"A guy that had flesh on his bones." She's down to a whisper. Her hands span the generous width of an invisible being. "Someone big enough to hang onto."

I sit back on my haunches. Bernie and I have entered territory seriously more important than a cucumber harvest. "I didn't know you liked beefy guys. Like the guy from Meatloaf? That big?"

Bernie flashes me a thumbs up. "But that's between you, me, and the cucumber patch."

I look across the alfalfa field and get used to the idea of Bernie and Meatloaf. After my gag reflex settles, I start picking again. That's the thing about people's hidden desires. Once they're out in the open, they're not such a big deal.

"I bet John always shares his Chiclets," Bernie says, back to snapping off cukes.

"Every time." I leave the barbed heart behind and shuffle ahead. John MacIntosh, my boyfriend with the angel curls at the back of his neck, shares everything. Except my appreciation for art. I'm feeling wistful and alone in the matter when an engine rumbles in the distance.

A pick-up truck, hot pepper red and bursting with orangey flames painted on the doors, pulls into Bernie's laneway. The truck bounces down the gravel path past the Schellenbergers' bungalow and rusted swing set, past their steel chicken barn, and stops at the edge of the field. A girl in her twenties climbs out and tramps across the field, her hips swaying back and forth like her bones aren't screwed in tight enough. "What in hell is that?" I mutter to Bernie.

"Looking for your dad," the girl calls out after she's strutted in close enough for us to hear. She's swinging a book, a big gold one, and her jeans are rolled up to just above her knees. Knobby, goaty things. An elaborate design is painted on her pant leg, like her clothes got tattooed.

"Check the hair," I say to Bernie. "Looks like she cut the mangle with her eyes closed." She hasn't squandered her life poring over *Seventeen* magazines, that's for sure.

"One of your dads, anyway," the girl calls. Upon closer inspection, it's plain that Bernie and I are not sisters. I'm what our gym teacher calls an ectomorph. She once asked if I could provide an illustration of skinny and flat. *Could you stand up for us Martha?* Then there's my neck. The guy behind me in math once called me a giraffe. And could I reach the upper leaves when foraging? There was a crabapple tree in his back yard that needed trimming. The trouble with a long neck is that you always look like you're straining. Not for leaves, but for something.

"Dad's in town," Bernie says. "Didn't think you'd get here so early."

The girl oversteps our leafy path of plants and pats her book. It's a photo album swirled in paisley, like the one we bought from Zellers for my sister's wedding.

"I brought my portfolio to show your family," she says, too much in a hurry to smile. She eyes Bernie's garden gloves, wet with dirt and tinged in army green, and hugs her album tighter. "I'll leave this on the porch," she adds crisply. "You can look at it later."

A portfolio. Like for art. I squeeze in front of Bernie. The gold paisley on the cover dances in the sun.

Bernie pulls off her gloves. "Can't we see your paintings now? Martha's probably interested, right Martha? Oh." She looks at the girl. "This is ... what was your name? Satin?"

"Velvet." She enunciates carefully. "Velvet Rudder."

Velvet. I could use a handle as cool as that. I was named after some chick in the Bible who got stuck doing everyone's housework.

"Velvet is painting a sign for our front lawn," Bernie says. "*Schellenberger Farms*, it'll say. *Norm, Barb and Bernadette.*"

I edge closer to the paisley. I could dive into its swirls.

Velvet backs up a step. "I'll pick up the album on Monday."

"You don't even have a minute to show us?" I try to sound casual. Friendly, but not desperate.

Velvet checks her rumbling truck in the distant laneway. She sighs. "One minute and that's all." She opens her album and props the spine against a fencepost, and Bernie and I lean in for the privilege of viewing her signs. Signs on front lawns, on barns and standing in fields. Oval ones mostly, bearing the names of horse farms and hog barns. A feed company. A dairy. They're hand painted, and proud like Bernie's nose.

"So artistical!" Bernie says.

"Nice work," I say, but the words come out like a croak. Velvet is making zesty, beautiful signs, while I'm picking six to ten bushels of cukes a day for pickles that'll be slopped on burgers and swallowed by billions of carnivores. Forget the sweat trickling down my front. Something dark and acidic is seeping in. Envy.

"I can make traditional rectangular signs," Velvet says, "but the oval ones are more unique. Egg-like in a way, which when you think about it, is … life giving."

"Oh, I love the oval ones." Bernie nods earnestly.

You could scratch your name in the dirt with a stick and Bernie would be first up for the standing ovation, but she's right about Velvet's signs. Oval-shaped or not, they're practically alive. She stretches some letters tall and squishes other ones into squatting things waddling across a line. Stands single letters off on their own or bunches them tight into families, squabbling for space.

"I think of signs as portraits," Velvet says. Her minute with us expired long ago, but she doesn't seem to care anymore. "Graphic likenesses that express one's personality. You can shout out the name of a farm with straight-from-the-can orange and bold faced letters. Or you may need a sign that isn't more than a whisper." She simmers down. "A hush of blue on white for the quiet, sensitive person, whose voice is faint but sure." She looks at me and nods. Whether she's feeling agreeable about her vision or she thinks she's pegged me, I don't know, but I pull my eyes from hers and return to the opened page.

Then I see it: the typed style "g" is flipped the wrong way. "That letter isn't backwards, is it?" I point to the letter to demonstrate my attentiveness to visual details.

As Velvet yanks the album close and examines the letter, her tufts of hair seem to spike out more violently. "The letter is set just as it should be." She slaps the book closed. "Takes years of experience to develop an eye for lettering and trust me, I've had years." She catches Bernie's eye and says, "Is your friend a cucumber picker or a nitpicker?"

I swallow.

"Actually, Martha's an artist too," Bernie says.

"I just fool around."

Bernie smiles hopeful encouragement. Velvet sends a sideways scowl. With the sun blasting down on me, my skin burns hotter than ever. But deep inside me, the need to confess my full colour dreams come surging up and clanging at the base of my throat—and not the flatbed dream either, but the other one. The one about ditching this dust bowl I call home and launching my training and eventual career as an urban artist of high regard. Except Velvet Rudder will dissolve into laughter, slap her painted jeans and clutch her bony chest to keep from falling over. "I don't make anything special," I end up muttering.

"Can't hear you," Velvet says.

Louder, I say, "I said, I don't make anything all pulled together like your collection of signs." I dig the toe of my runner under a clod of dirt.

"That's not true." Bernie turns to Velvet. "You could say Martha's pencil case is a kind of masterpiece, the way she doodles lines all over it with a couple of magic markers."

"Nonobjective art?" Velvet covers a yawn with the back of her hand. "I did that back in Toronto."

Damn Bernie.

"How was it for you there?" Bernie asks in a tone of deepest sympathy.

"Oh, I love the city. The art scene is fabulous. But I'm not interested in abstractions anymore. I believe the noblest art is both functional and aesthetically pleasing. And above all, an honest expression of the truth."

"Martha doesn't make useful art," Bernie admits.

"Thanks, Bern." I try to chuckle, but Velvet doesn't look amused. The cucumber field goes as silent as the gymnasium during a final exam. An exam you're failing, bad.

Velvet checks her watch again and holds her photo album aloft like a sacred manuscript. "I'll set this on your porch. Have a look through with your parents." She looks past me like I'm no more important than a fencepost. I return to my cucumber row, sink back to my haunches and lift a vine.

"And if either of you like," Velvet continues, "you could make rough sketches for the sign over the weekend. I need an idea of what you want."

I drop the vine, along with my shriveled hopes for coming clean with my dreams. But when the vine hits the ground, it forms a kind of question mark, and I wonder. Could Velvet Rudder overlook her distaste for pencil case doodles, nonobjective art and me in general? Could she lead me into the world of art and artists?

"I'll come by Monday and see what you've dreamed up," Velvet adds. Her attention shifts to her still rumbling truck. I open my mouth to utter a promise about providing a dizzying array of lettering possibilities, but fear clogs my throat. Velvet turns her goaty knees and tattooed jeans away from us.

"I could do up sketches," I finally blurt out, but even Bernie doesn't hear me.

Chapter 2

THAT NIGHT, I WARM UP for the Schellenberger design by lettering my name. I draw on the floor of my bedroom, if you can call it that. The room used to be a choir loft when our place was a church. Decades ago, the congregation emptied out. The place went dusty and lonely until eight years ago when my parents discovered the church, a lost soul they could save. We live in a building shaped like an oversized doghouse but with tall windows, pointed at the top. The church sits just outside the sign for Putnam. It looks like it wanted to get into the village, but got cut from the team.

I draw dreamy bubble shapes for "Martha" until my mind drifts ahead to Monday morning. I'll stand by the door of Velvet's truck and pass her a folder bursting with sketches. The first page will have a drawing for Bernie's family, but I'll show her other ideas too. Sign ideas for dress shops, hair salons, and a florist. Even a *patisserie*, because a French baker I met on a Quebec trip is interested in my work, I'll say. Once Velvet regains her ability to speak, she'll say my ideas are "whimsical yet strong." I'll blush like a fool, and then she'll insist we paint my design for the Schellenbergers.

The phone rings beside my bed.

"Got back from Ridley Township," John says. "It's hilly up there but acreage is cheap." John is such a farm boy he could play Pa's kid brother on *Little House on the Prairie*. He even has the dark curls and field-worked muscles. Steady, strong hands, too, not that we've ventured far into the forest of physical desire, although we've found ourselves wandering around its edges. And believe me, the forest is inviting.

"Hold on," I say. My dad, waiting to hear about a job, is calling upstairs.

"It's just Bernie!" I lie loudly, even though my parents like John, who has all the time in the world to chat about farming trends. He can go on and on until I forget to pay attention and imagine us sinking into the horizon. Then I thunk the side of my brain and remind myself we don't need to make commitments we'll regret later.

"What's wrong with telling your dad it's me?" John says.

"He's been asking too many questions," I whisper. "About our level of intimacy. I'm pretending I don't know what he's talking about. I think it's working."

"Did you tell him we never get time alone?"

"I did, and he said, 'Oh my apologies, Martha. Why don't your mother and I take a week's holiday in Tampa and give you two time to yourselves?'"

John sighs. "Anyway, when I was up in Ridley, I got an idea for my next story."

Before he graduated, John wrote agriculturally based sci-fi stories for the school newspaper. Kids made alien jokes behind his back. Once someone passed us in the halls and started whistling the Star Wars song.

"It came to me," he continues. "A futuristic society grows their harvest in space labs, and drops it to Earth in packages."

"Cool, John." He lost me after "futuristic," but I have my sketching. I shade a letter with crosshatching.

"You don't think it's horrific?"

"Cool-horrific." I should have told him I'm not a sci-fi fan months ago, but I didn't want to hurt his feelings, and now it's too late.

"Did you finish reading my last story about the cows?"

"On Mars. Nice one. I liked the interplanetary dairy exchange."

John would give me his stories to read before he put them in the paper. They were always handwritten, with the words pressed deep into the page. No margins or indenting. No space for a girl to breathe, especially because his hero guy always had a lover pledging her everlasting adoration. I crosshatch a little harder.

"Why don't you come over on Sunday?" John says, and right away his baritone softens my hatching. "Have dinner with us. My parents might take the boys swimming after. Could be just you and me."

I set my pencil aside. "That could be fun. How long would they be gone?" It's important for John and I to make the most of our summer. In the fall, he's leaving for university.

"Not long enough, but it's something."

"I'll see what I can do." I close the notebook and lower my volume. "Last night I had this fantasy." I've been willing to venture into the great forest of physical desire—and I mean deep into the forest—all summer, but John wants us to take our time. To enjoy the journey.

"Go on."

"You probably won't like it." I pull the quilt off my bed and over my head, tent like, to muffle my voice from curious ears downstairs.

"Try me."

In the darkness of my quilt-tent, I picture John's Crest-white teeth shining from five miles away. John has highly developed personal hygiene. "No one's on another line? What about your brothers?"

"They're playing hockey in the driveway. We're fine."

"I had this fantasy," I repeat. "Did you just close your door?"

"Yeah."

"Of painting you with a brush dipped in a mud bath. I saw a picture of one of those places in a National Geographic. From Spain or something."

"Mud, huh?"

I can practically hear his forehead crinkling. "I knew you wouldn't like it."

"Wouldn't the mud dry up? Make your skin feel cracked and dusty?"

"But we wash it off. In the pond, with a wet sponge."

"With algae floating around?"

I toss the quilt off. "Forget I mentioned anything."

"We could skip the mud. You could lather me up with soap foam."

"You'd look like a sheep."

"A ram, Martha," he says, all manly. "Fine. Paint the mud."

"Seriously? John MacIntosh, who takes two showers a day—"

"Three if I have to—"

"Would get muddy for me?" I pull the quilt around me again.

"For you."

"God, John. You really do like me." Sometimes I wonder if I deserve someone as nice as him.

"How many times do I have to tell you? So could you get the car or should I pick you up?"

I have no respect for girls who date guys for their cars, but it just so happens that John has his own. "Could you pick me up?"

"Sure. If there's time, we could swing past the Ridley property. The land is hilly, but it's workable."

"Damn." I flub a letter and reach for my worn nub of Pink Pearl eraser. "Lettering is harder than it looks."

"What lettering?"

"Just my name."

"I think it goes like this: M ... A ... R—"

"I'm practicing, John. Working out designs for Bernie's sign. Her family is getting one painted."

"You're making the sign?"

"I'm helping with the design." Being able to say that feels so right. I shade a letter with the side of my pencil. Make it full and plump.

"Who's painting it?"

"This girl."

"Who?"

"Velvet something."

"Rudder?" he says. "With the red truck?"

"You know her?" I stop shading.

"No, but the neighbours got her to paint a sign."

"And?"

"Apparently, she's crazy."

I groan. I love how people believe whatever anyone says. "Why would you say that?"

"She's emotional. High strung. Likes things to go her way. I heard she lived in T.O. for a while. Maybe that messed her up."

"Living in Toronto?" John's been there maybe two whole times.

"The place is a zoo."

"Listen, John." I struggle to keep irritation out of my voice. "Maybe I shouldn't come tomorrow. I've got work to do." I peer down at my deflated bubble letters.

"It's just a sketch for a sign. Finish it tonight." He clears his throat. "Ridley Township has a lot going for it, you know." Something about trolling fields satisfies him, but I have serious designing to do.

"You might be very interested in a particular property," he adds.

I sigh. "Call me in the morning. I'll let you know if I have time."

After we hang up, I flip the page so I don't have to look at my godawful bubble letters. How can I spare a second from my work? I grab the eraser and start in on a new design.

THAT NIGHT AT DINNER, I take my seat on the pine pew and drag it closer to my plate, set on the antique communion table with "In Remembrance of Me" carved on its side. Sopranos howl choral music at full volume from the stereo. My parents think the religious stuff adds to the flavour of our house. To keep the churchy feeling, they didn't divide the space into rooms. "Open concept," my dad calls it, although he and Mom get a door on their bedroom, where the church office used to be.

Mom sets down a plate of roast pork and a bowl of salad. "Gerald," she shouts over a crescendo, "the music is a bit loud!"

"What's that?" my dad yells from his desk, which is under my bedroom loft.

"Too loud!" Mom shouts. "And supper—"

"Ah!" says Dad. He springs out of his chair, lowers the volume on the stereo, and rubs his hands together. "Smells wonderful!" My dad is a big man. Not in an all over Meatloaf kind of way, but tall, with a pillow-sized paunch he sucks in and pats like he's going to have to deal with that soon, when he's not shifting the hair thinning at the back of his head. He seats himself and bows his head in prayer. Mom and I copy.

"Come, Lord Jesus," Dad says.

I close my eyes. Every drawing I made upstairs was worse than the one before.

"Be our guest," he continues.

Half the weekend is gone and I have nothing decent to show Velvet.

"Let these gifts …"

I wonder if it's worse to show her crappy drawings or nothing at all.

"To us be blessed. Amen."

No. I grip my praying hands together. I have to show Velvet something. Anything. I can't give up the chance to work with a real artist.

"Amen," Mom adds and pushes a runaway lock of greying hair behind her ear.

"Pork?" Dad presents the plate to me like he roasted the pig himself.

"Martha made friends with an artist yesterday," Mom says, smoothing her napkin on her lap.

"I didn't say she's a friend, Mom. I just met her."

"What artist?" Dad says.

"Some girl." Who can show me the truth and the way if I manage to draw something that isn't the visual equivalent of fingernails on a blackboard. "Bernie's family is hiring her to paint a sign for their lawn."

"I read about her," Mom says. Her best friend is the local newspaper. "She's got a nice business going."

"Who cares about some other artist?" Dad says. "When will the papers write about you, Martha? When are you going to stop squirreling away your drawings and make a splash?"

"I'm not an artist, Dad. I just draw sometimes."

"It's all about attitude, Martha. Change your attitude, change your life. Exude confidence and people will believe in you." He leans over and taps my back. "And sit up straight."

I haul my spine to attention.

"Change your attitude, change your life." Dad draws the words out long. "That's it, Peggy. The title for my next seminar!"

Mom looks like she wants to say something, but stops herself. "Sounds promising," she finally says, and saws her meat into tiny pieces.

My dad used to be a minister, but he gave up the collar ten years ago. Now he's leading positive thinking workshops for anyone who's feeling down, especially the ones who can afford his fee.

"Doesn't matter whether you're selling Bibles, frying pans or signs," Dad continues. "You have to talk yourself up. Why are the Schellenbergers hiring someone else to paint their sign anyway? Tell them you'll do it. Tell them you can start right away." His eyes sparkle.

"I'm helping with design ideas. I'll show them to Velvet on Monday."

"Velvet? The other artist?" Dad waves the thought of her away. "Martha. Think about it. It's Norm who needs to see your design. You want to be an artist? Snap up the jobs. Quick." He grabs an invisible offer from the air, just above my glass of milk.

"I don't know anything about sign painting."

Dad slops extra gravy on his pork and rolls his eyes like what is my problem? "Call Norm. Call him now and say, 'Mr. Schellenberger.'" He slows down his speech, should I care to take notes. "'I understand you need a sign for your lawn. I would be happy to paint it for you.' Find out exactly what the other girl charges, and charge the same. No. Charge more. Charge more and he'll know you're better."

"Martha doesn't know how to paint signs, Gerald," Mom says.

"I've never worked that big."

"Paint is paint," Dad says.

"Let Martha sort things out herself." Mom presses her hand over Dad's wrist.

He gives her hand a rub. "People around here will pay anything to tart up the look of their farms, Martha. You can be the one to do it. On-the-job-training is all you need. Shall I call Norm for you? Should we buy you supplies?"

"Gerald," Mom says. The worry lines engraved between her eyebrows huddle closer together.

I sit up taller and try and block Dad's view of the phone, dangerously close. Bernie's parents, already generous hosts for our cucumber business, will wonder what the hell got into my family, thinking we can help ourselves to any employment on their farm we take a fancy to.

"Not that painting signs would be considered a true art form," Dad tells my mother and me, the last remaining members of his congregation. "But sign painting may be just the thing for you, Martha." Suddenly, Dad casts his gaze toward the ceiling. "Now Leonardo da Vinci. There's an artist."

Saved by the master.

"Do you think he shied away from a commission?" Dad continues. "*The Last Supper*. Remember *The Last Supper*, Peggy?" My mother is actually better informed in art history, but he forgets.

"Of course," she says.

"The painting where Jesus announces that someone in the room will betray him? You can see that crafty Judas in the shadows, the one who will betray the great teacher. Where's that book, Peggy? Show Martha *The Last Supper*."

"I think it's on the bottom shelf." Mom sets down her fork.

"I've seen the painting," I say. "But I don't remember what Judas looked like." Best to keep Dad elevated with his lofty thoughts of da Vinci.

"It's fascinating how the artist captures the disciple's thoughts in light and dark." With his knife, Dad carves a line in the air from some remembered detail of the painting, and gazes at it.

Mom, house reference librarian and financier for Dad's passing interests, is still chewing but bent before the bookshelves. While she's there, Dad gives the air a punch for his latest eureka. "I've got it. A sign for your signs. Paint a sign advertising your business, and we'll post it on the front lawn! Come up with a catchy name. How about, 'Fine Signage?'"

"I've never painted a sign," I say. "I'm not ready to advertise."

"Peggy," Dad calls. "We need to invest in wood for Martha." He passes his hands over an imaginary panel. "Something classy. That boyfriend of yours could cut it to size. Where's he been lately, anyway?"

"Checking out land or something. I don't know. It's not like I talk to him every day. It's casual."

"Good. At your age, casual is exactly where you want to be." Dad shoots me a double barrelled look for reinforcement and adds, "You're not wearing eye pencil, are you?" He frowns, like he just bit into some gristle.

"Not really."

"Let's not rush into buying paint supplies, Gerald," says Mom. She's returned with a fat book flopping over her arms and open to *The Last Supper*.

"It's an exciting investment," Dad says.

Mom has a small but comfortable inheritance from her Great Aunt Bernice. Dad has all kinds of ideas for making her money grow, but sometimes I think they're costing more than they're earning.

Mom opens the book wider. "Anyway, here's the painting."

"Speaking of suppers," says Dad, "I invited a seminary student to dinner Sunday. You can whip something up, can't you?" He smiles at Mom.

"What seminary student?" Mom's napkin disappears inside her fist and limps out a moment later, destroyed.

"A relative of a man in my last seminar. Fine man. His niece is moving here from Winnipeg to train for the ministry at Wellington. I had to help, Peggy. The man is well connected with management at the Holiday Inn. He could get me a discounted conference room for seminars."

Mom gathers the crumpled napkin in her fist. "I won't have time to buy groceries."

"Renting space at the Holiday Inn could be a big break, Peggy. Worth an extra run to the store, don't you think?"

Mom chews in silence.

Dad looks into the distance, out one of our tall, gothic windows and adds, "'Fine Signage.' Not a bad name at all."

I squirm in my pew.

"Just stay clear of your competition, Martha. Nab that commission at the Schellenbergers before it's too late. And if it is too late? Then by golly," Dad punches the communion table with his fist, "I'll hire you to paint a sign. And that's a promise."

My shoulders fall. "I can't paint a professional sign for anyone right now, Dad. I don't know how—"

Dad holds up his hand. "We're a can-do family, Martha."

"Fine. I'll ask Norm," I say. "But—"

"Excellent, Martha!" Dad cheers a victory fist. "I sense a change in you. A new willingness to take chances."

I search Mom's eyes for help, but she's too busy scribbling a grocery list on her rumpled napkin to notice.

Chapter 3

SUNDAY MORNING, I WAKE UP EARLY and quietly search for paper in my desk drawer. Choir lofts are meant to carry sound, but I don't want to alert the snoring parents. I rifle through crunched report cards and crooked sketches of Kurt Cobain and Madonna, pause over Madonna, and then drop her into the garbage. I need to make my drawings bigger. Bolder. More carefully considered, like Velvet's signs and *The Last Supper*.

I root past pencil stubs and bent paperclips, but I can only find flimsy bond paper that'll rip the second I erase a line. With what could blossom into a full hour uninterrupted by a thundering Bach concerto or prods to dust the pipe organ, I have to sketch like hell. Forget the Duo-Tang busting with possibilities. There's no hope for that. I'll just make one perfect drawing. Velvet will be so awestruck by the talent radiating from my paper that she'll ask me to work with her. Dad doesn't need to know.

Then I slide it out. A single, virgin white sheet of blank paper, respectable in weight. "Crap," I blurt out. One of Dad's old sermons is photocopied on the other side. I don't want Velvet Rudder to mistake me for a religious freak.

For support, I lay the otherwise perfect sheet on a hardcover book, *How to Sketch Horses the Easy Way*, and position myself belly down on the floor. After yesterday's drawing warm up, I can pull off this baby. I've been dreaming about Bernie's sign since four in the morning and this time I'm not making dopey balloon letters.

With a ruler, I pencil a sure line to mark the top of the design. I'll make Norm's metal barn grow from one letter. I mark a baseline. A chicken will peek over another. I'll perch a steaming plate of scrambled eggs on the final letter. I tuck hair behind my ear and ignore my father's footsteps clunking out from the bedroom. And when the letters are done, I'll weave cucumber vines, ripe with vegetables and fringed in tendrils, around the frame of the sign, for a plan that will knock Velvet Rudder's hand painted socks off.

LATER THAT AFTERNOON, I wait by the front door. John is still next to my dad at the dinner/communion table, which is set with an extra plate. My mother is banging pots in the kitchen in an angry frenzy. The seminary student is visiting today. I had to vacuum the rugs and dust the altar we use for setting out coffee cups. The chores cut my sketching time down to almost nothing, but I've got a rough drawing at least. A rough rough. It's weird how perfect ideas in your mind can look so different in real life.

I agreed to dinner at John's, as long as I could rush home to rework the plate of scrambled eggs. In no time, my virgin sheet got violated by a fit of eraser marks. The drawing looks like scratches from a five year old boy with a grudge against schoolwork.

John is still wearing his John Deere cap. "Ridley Township isn't more than a quarter of an hour's drive north of here," he tells my dad. "Reasonably priced, but still good for cash cropping."

I tap an anxious beat with my thumbnail on the door handle.

Dad leans over the table, strokes his chin and listens. "If land is that cheap, I should buy acreage." He holds up a hand as if to silence John while the light bulb in his brain illuminates. "I could build a conference facility." He leans back and stretches both arms to a full wingspan to frame the imaginary building.

"For your positive thinking seminars?" John asks.

The pot clanging from the kitchen stops. "Where would we get that kind of money, Gerald?" Mom calls.

My dad says quietly to John, "That's *negative* thinking," and returns to regular volume. "My seminars could be the beginning. A cornerstone to the instructional aspect of the facility. But I wouldn't stop there."

Dad's business has been slow. His stream of souls awaiting motivation hasn't been flowing so well, but the excitement in his eye is still shining.

"I picture the place as a resort-slash-conference centre," he continues, "with not only corporate leadership seminars, but an indoor swimming pool and exercise centre to promote fitness in all endeavors."

"In Ridley Township?" John asks.

I've been there. Nothing but fields and a few chipped stone houses.

"Absolutely." Smiling like a game show host, Dad twists toward the front door. "Martha! You could paint signs for my centre. *Five miles ahead. On your right. Welcome to Seminars for Success.*" His eyes go dreamy.

"You've got quite the ideas," John says.

I wiggle the screen door handle. "What time are we eating, John?" I'll never get home in time to rework my design.

He checks the cuckoo clock hanging above the altar. "Keep thinking, Gerald." He gives Dad a thumbs up and pushes his pew back. "Martha and I should go. I'll have her home by eight."

"Hmm," Dad says, back to stroking his chin while John and I slip out the front door. As the handle catches, Dad sprints up to the screen.

"Casual, Martha," he calls out the door. "Just like we talked about!"

I wave goodbye, and we pull out of the driveway in John's Datsun.

TEN MINUTES LATER, John rumbles the car along a path that snakes into a wooded area, part of the extra acreage his family owns. He pulls off the dirt road, shuts the engine and slides close to me, a welcome distraction from the stress of designing a masterful sign. His hat has tipped off and his hair, hot and damp already, smells like Ivory soap. The knob of gearshift is driving into my thigh, but who cares? John's warm tongue is circling my ear. My finger is tracing the edge of his underwear peeking over his jeans, and our stomachs are sliding against each other. We pulled up our shirts for better contact.

"We won't be too late for dinner, will we?" I say as he works at the button of my shirt.

John tilts my head so he can see the clock on the dash and then smacks his own back against the seat. "The grapefruit is on the table already."

"Where did your mother get the idea of grapefruit for an appetizer anyway?"

John pulls himself back to me, and slips his hand along my leg. "With a maraschino cherry on top?"

His dinner table is another world away.

"She got the idea from my aunt." Quickly, John pulls his hand away. "We have to go."

"Damn."

"I know."

We pull our shirts back down, and I smooth my hair. The car makes its backing up singing screech as we reverse from our pine scented, wooded wonderland. John revs to highway speed and I dig my hand between his thigh and the seat to prolong some of our body pressure. As his leg leans into my hand, I try and flash freeze the memory of his stomach against mine so I can recreate it later, like my mother does with strawberries so she can thaw them out and have a juicy memory of spring whenever she likes.

"I should have said I'd bring you home for nine." John raps the steering wheel with the heel of his hand. "I had your dad right where I wanted him. Now there's no time to drive up to Ridley."

"I have to come home early anyway, remember? To work on my design."

"You're not finished that thing yet?"

"Just the warm ups, rough roughs and a good rough." I gaze past his dangling air freshener and try not to think about how to turn my fury of erasure marks into a beauteous string of letters. "Drawing a complex design takes a serious amount of work," I explain.

"I'm sure." Fields and fence lines swish past us.

"Excuse me?" I can't help it, but I sound like a strung out supply teacher.

"I get it, Martha. Sometimes when I write a story, I have to sit and think about it for a few minutes."

"That's it? You sit for a few minutes, the words spill out and you're done? Wham, bam, thank you ma'am?"

"Pretty much. Except once I changed an ending. The writing is just for fun. It's not like real work."

John could scrawl a billion sci-fi stories and he'd still never understand the challenges of making visual art. "You know what, John? My stomach feels queasy." It isn't even a lie.

He checks his rear view. "Want me to pull over?"

"No. But I think I need to go back home." Taking an evening off was the stupidest idea ever.

"Now?"

Maybe my stomach doesn't feel that bad, but my head is a wreck, and I can't handle John's attitude. "You can have my grapefruit."

He heaves a sigh and gears down, thank God, pulls onto the gravel shoulder and swings the car around. "When you're feeling better, we'll take a drive up to Ridley."

"What is it with that place?"

"It's just peaceful. I like it there."

"Whatever turns you on." I peer out the side window. Then I wonder if John has sourced out a prime spot for having sex or something, which could be extremely romantic once I let his bad attitude go. With the car pointed toward home, already my stomach is unclenching. Soon I'll get my hands on my sixty pack of Laurentians and transform the scrambled eggs into technicolour.

WHEN I RETURN HOME, Mom is sitting stiffly on one pew and Dad and some goofy-looking girl are chuckling across the communion table. If dreams came true, I'd slide in the front door, slink upstairs unnoticed, and find my pencil crayons.

"Martha," Dad calls as I slip off my sandals. "You're home early! We just finished dinner. Come. I want you to meet someone!"

I trudge over and sit next to my mom, whose hair looks greyer than usual and wilted around her neck.

"This is Debbie, Ned McKellar's niece," Dad says. "She's here from Winnipeg and she just finished reading a book on positive affirmations. Can you believe it?"

"Well, hi there!" Debbie smiles and her oversized teeth come out shining. The corners of her mouth are saliva-wet. She's got a massive head, like a Great Dane's.

"Hi." I remember to sound unwell and glance at my mother. "I'm not feeling that great. I might go up to my room."

"Oh?" Concern clouds Debbie's face. "What's wrong? Is it a girl problem?"

Dad clears his throat. "I'm sure it's nothing. Martha gets stomach aches sometimes. She's our artist, Debbie."

"I love your bedroom," Debbie says.

Sweet Jesus. "You went up there?"

"Dad and Debbie did," Mom says, her shoulders pinched together.

"Your dad was explaining the architecture of the house," Debbie says. "It is *wondrous* that you live in a church. I love that organ! And the hymn numbers on the wall? So fun."

"Debbie is about to begin her training in the ministry," Dad says.

"I heard." I tap a fingernail on the pew. "How long did you stay in my room?"

"Not long," Debbie says. "Don't worry. We didn't snoop. But since your drawings for the Kellenberger signs—"

"Schellenberger," my mother corrects quietly.

"—were lying all over the floor," Debbie continues, "we had a look. Wow." She nods slowly and earnestly. "You really worked hard on those."

"You looked at my drawings?" I tame an urge to snatch the brass collection plate from the middle of the table and knock it over her head.

"We did," Debbie says. "And there's nothing wrong with any of your drawings. I've got a bit of an eye for design myself. I adore taking pictures. Not that our efforts have to be anything special for God to appreciate them. As long as you try, that's the important thing." Her smile disappears and she nods deeply.

"I'm going to pour myself something." Mom stands and heads for the cupboard under the sink, even though she rarely touches alcohol.

"Reverend Gerald has promised to help me with my efforts at becoming a minister," Debbie says to me.

Reverend Gerald?

"It's great to have someone I can read scripture with," she adds. "I can't even believe I got into university! I'm really excited about deepening my understanding of what it means to be a minister and speaking up on behalf of the Lord. It's kind of exciting and scary at the same time, you know what I mean?"

If she took my Madonna drawing out of the garbage, I'll strangle her.

"I've decided to give Debbie all my past sermons as study material. When a protégé finds a mentor, new beginnings can bear fruit," Dad says.

If I can't show Velvet a decent design, my hopes at a mentor are shot.

Debbie bares her happy-teeth again. "Not sure what all that means, but it sounds good to me!"

"Oh, Debbie. Remember?" Dad jabs his head toward the space on the pew beside her.

"Right! I nearly forgot. As for your drawings, Reverend Gerald and I thought it would be fun to have a kind of judging contest to decide which of your sketches is the best one."

Or I could crash the pipe organ over top of her. I hold my fists in my lap.

"This is the one we picked." Debbie looks down at the pew and pulls out a sheet of paper. My paper. My drawing on the virgin page.

"My sketch," I cry out. My good rough, with the chicken and the scrambled eggs.

"Don't worry. It didn't take us long to choose," Debbie says.

"It's got coffee stains all over it." I snatch the drawing and pull it close.

"Sorry. Reverend Gerald and I were having so much fun, I spilled my cup. But you can still see all the little details, like that dish at the end of ... what is it? Cream of Wheat? What a cute idea!"

I stand up and grip the edge of the pew. "They're scrambled eggs," I say through gritted teeth. "I'm going to my room. Because I. Am. Not. Feeling. Well." I march past the kitchen, past my mother sipping a small glass of sherry normally reserved for guests, and stomp up the stairs.

I overhear Debbie say, "Do you think we should have chosen another picture?"

"Doesn't matter," Dad says quietly. "She's feeling a little tense. Martha's pitching her new idea to the Schellenbergers tomorrow."

"She's showing them *that* sketch?" Debbie says, forgetting to whisper. "Well good luck to her."

I hurl the stupid drawing in the garbage with Madonna and throw myself on my bed.

Chapter 4

MONDAY MORNING I OVERSLEEP because the battery on my god-damn alarm betrays me on the most important day of my life. I lean over the balcony and check the clock downstairs. Twenty past eight. I was supposed to be at Bernie's two hours ago. I rip off my pajamas and lunge for the gardening clothes still heaped on the floor since Friday. Velvet could be at Bernie's at any minute. I might have missed her already.

In the morning light, my drawing looks worse than ever. After Debbie left last night, I ironed most of the crumples out, which left a toasted scorch in the top right corner. The coffee stain isn't going anywhere and looks more like blood that won't wash out of your underwear, but under all that, my drawing is still there. Maybe it's not my best work, but I was too tired and hungry to make anything else. And I don't care if Dorkey thinks the drawing is the best from a pile of crap. She's a stranger from left field I'll never see again. Velvet Rudder's opinion is the one that matters.

"You're late," Bernie says, after I drop my bike on her front lawn and power walk to the field. She points to the drawing under my arm. "Is that it?"

"Is this what?"

"Your sketch for our sign." Bernie's garden gloves are already damp and dirty.

"How did you know?"

"Didn't your dad tell you? He phoned over."

"Aw, geeze."

"He said to prepare ourselves for a truly incredible sign design."

"He shouldn't have stuck his nose in."

"Martha." Bernie's voice is calm. She sets a cucumber down and slips her arm under mine, like she's got bad news to break. "My parents left for town already, but they told me to let you know. They're set with hiring ... you know. That other girl." She shakes her head.

"I don't care, Bernie." I wrench my arm back. "I just want to see Velvet."

"But your dad—"

"To hell with my dad. Where's Velvet?" I grip my drawing tight. I couldn't cram it into my pocket, and sticking it in a photo album would've been copying, so I glued it onto a square of cardboard from the back of a Cheerios box. At least the photocopied sermon is hidden. The cardboard was all I could find at midnight, but as long as the yellow side is face down, no one will see.

"She stopped by a while ago."

Panic surges up my throat. "When did she leave?" All my work could be for nothing.

Bernie puts her hands on her hips and arches her back to ease her muscles for the longest stretch in the history of cucumber picking. "Just a few minutes ago."

"Where was she going?" I snap.

"I wouldn't know. Wait. She said something about stopping at the store for corn chips."

"Good work, Bernie!" I throw my arms around her.

"What's the big rush?" Bernie calls as I make a run for my bike. "Can't you stay a few minutes? There's something I need to tell you about."

"I owe you, Bernie. I'll pick the entire next row," I call back, and run harder to the edge of the field.

I hop on my rusted ten speed, plow past the barn and the house, and skid out from Bernie's gravel laneway, sending stones flying. My front tire slips on the loose gravel and I wind up beside Bernie's mailbox and sprawled across my toppled bike. Its front wheel spins crazily. My leg is scraped and spouting blood from dusty openings. But this time, thank the Lord above and the heavens and all that, the drawing is spared. I stand and lift up my bike. Miraculously, although the front fork is bent, it still works.

I pedal past the French fry truck parked a mile this side of Putnam, and finally reach the village. I scan past Lucky's—the general store, and past the dirty Buick idling out front, until my eyes land on a red truck with painted flames. Velvet Rudder climbs inside. Her shoulder bends forward as she reaches into the shadows of the cab to turn on the ignition. *Almost there, Velvet.* I pump my pedals hard along the wide street, each motion sending stabs of pain down my leg, which is weeping red.

She turns to check behind her. Reverses the truck. *Wait, Velvet. I'm coming.* I'm biking one-handed with my drawing clamped in my armpit. I know I'm soaking another liquid onto it, but that can't be helped. I'm so close I can see the tufts of Velvet's hair, spiking laser jabs out from her head. I squeeze the hand brake, but can't stop.

My bike skids on the pavement. A gruesome thud shakes the front wheel and sends a jolt up my spine.

Velvet opens her window and sticks her head out. "What in hell are you doing?"

I lower tiptoes to the asphalt and shimmy the bike backwards. "I'm so very, highly, extremely sorry." I can't find any more words.

She pulls open her door and climbs down. Assesses the damage, which is considerable. One of the orange flames painted on her door is dented into a dark and horrible cave.

Highly emotional, John described her. Likes to have things go her way.

"Some folks have exceptional insurance policies," she says, slowly. Her eyes flatten. "And others have cash to pay out. I don't know which one you are."

"I was hurrying to show you my drawing!"

"What drawing?"

"For the Schellenberger sign." I try to smile.

Velvet pulls her face back a notch to look at me fresh. "Who *are* you?"

"Martha." I ignore the disaster on the side of her truck and the blood dripping down my leg and push my shoulders back. "Martha Becker. The one with the pencil case."

"The what?"

"Remember? Bernie was saying my pencil case has lines drawn all over it."

I don't want to repeat the masterpiece part or I'll sound full of myself.

"You're the girl from the cucumber field?" Velvet still looks confused and not much happier.

"Yes! I came to show you my drawing." But when I reach for the sketch clamped in my armpit, nothing is there. I swing my head around and search the sidewalk in front of the store and past the two parked vehicles on Putnam's main street.

"Drawing, huh?" Velvet eyes me like I'm some kind of juvenile delinquent.

"It was right here. I was holding it."

She looks back at her dented truck door.

"There it is!" From under her truck, I see the corner of yellow peeking out. The Cheerios box was the best thing after all! I knew it.

"It's garbage," she says, like spitting isn't beneath her. "I'm getting tired—"

"Wait." I scramble off my bike, hunker down on all fours and strain my arm under the rumbling truck for my proof-of-artistic-effort. I hurry to a stand. Flip the cardboard over.

Velvet can't help herself, and I like that about her. She pulls my drawing in close. She's willing to look beyond the obstacles.

I wait. And wait, and wait as the front door of Lucky's chimes open and swings shut. A guy in coveralls climbs into his car, sinks away past B & K Tire and Battery down the street, and bends around the corner past Forbes Manufacturing, the chicken-cage factory. The sun, levitating in the east, casts hard light on my efforts with too many eraser marks, the burn, spilled coffee, dirt and sweat.

"You did this?" Velvet points to the breakfast dish, perched on the last letter. "What is this? Porridge?"

"No!" I fend off tears threatening to escape. "They're scrambled eggs."

"Oh. That was my next guess."

I hold my hand up. Use the other to press over my chest. My heart. "I wanted to help." Damn it to hell. My voice choked again.

"If you wanted to help," Velvet says, "why didn't you just say something? You didn't have to drive into my truck, for Christ's sake."

God. Oh, thank God. Velvet doesn't hate me. The tears are retreating. My throat and tongue are regaining strength. "I want to help," I say with conviction.

Velvet looks at the drawing again. Holds its corner and lets it dangle like someone else's snotty Kleenex. "This will not be the design of choice for the Schellenberger sign. But I can see you have a healthy—okay, maybe not healthy—but a hearty dose of commitment toward art, design and signage in general. Swing by my place over the next day or two. We'll talk." She nods at the blood snaking down my calf. "After you're cleaned up." She pulls a business card from her back pocket, cut by hand and a little jagged on one edge, and hands it to me.

"Really?" I accept the card like it's a robin's egg, small and wondrous. "I can come to your place?"

"That's what I said." She drums her fingers on the hood of the truck.

"Did you have a particular time slot in mind?"

"No." She sounds testy, maybe because of the truck repair in her future.

"That's okay." I can't stop smiling. "I can keep the timing loose. As for your truck, I can repay you in cucumber money."

A strange grin seems to float behind Velvet's lips. "We'll deal with the truck problem later."

I get a prickly feeling, like the kind you get from a yellow, diamond shaped danger sign at a tight turn on the highway. Maybe it's because of Velvet's odd smirk, or maybe because of Dad forbidding me to step into the competition's territory. Either way, I brush the feeling aside, because something more important is happening. I gaze toward the wide sky and inhale deeply. A real artist is accepting me into her life.

Chapter 5

THE NEXT DAY, after Bernie and I dump our day's harvest at the grading station, we return to her place. I curl up on the pink carpet in her living room. It's like I've sweated away the nine-ty-eight percent of my water and all that's left is a fetus-shaped raisin. A dried up useless raisin, when I could be bursting with life and art like Velvet Rudder. Picking cucumbers is sucking me dry, especially now that I'm on the brink of life as an artist.

I don't want to spring myself on Velvet right away or she'll think I'm desperate for artistic guidance. Hanging around Bernie's place is better. Besides, I'd rather savour my future with Velvet, like a wrapped gift waiting to be opened.

Bernie is on the floor too, pulling sweaters out of shopping bags and piling them beside the flowered couch. Nothing match-es in her living room except the recent date of manufacture. The big-ass stereo and glass topped coffee table are from this decade. Not like our place, where furniture is dated by the century.

Our friend Leanne sits on the couch with her arms sprawled wide. She's flat ironed her hair into cascading waves. Leanne is what my dad calls "a real looker." My mom gets nervous when I'm with her, like her tight T-shirts and Wild Cherry lip gloss might be catching and will infect my appearance. Not that I could look like Leanne if I tried.

"Come here, Martha." Leanne eyes me coiled up on the carpet. "I'll make you another set of earrings."

"Screw you," I say, but haul myself up to sitting. The last ones she Bic-penned on my earlobes were devil heads with horns.

"I'll make them pretty this time. I promise." She smiles sweetly and pats the flowered seat. "How about a cucumber design? Draw one for me. I'll copy it."

"I don't want cucumbers on my ears."

"Too phallic? But that could be fun."

"Phallic?" Bernie says, peeking over a sweater.

"Weenie like, Bern," I say. "You know. Penile. Of or pertaining to a penis?"

"Don't worry, Bernie. Some day your ship will come in." Leanne titters.

Bernie's forehead glows a shiny pink. "I knew what you meant. I just didn't know the word."

I remember not to mention Bernie's newly professed interest in beefy guys.

"We understand," Leanne says, like a Sunday school teacher. "Got anything to drink, Bern?"

"There's a case of Sprite."

"If that's all you've got. Hey, Bernie. Could you pick up a mickey of rum for Friday night?" Leanne adds, suddenly friendlier. The cashier who works Thursdays at the liquor store considers Bernie close enough to legal drinking age.

"I might stay home," Bernie says, her attention drilled into her sweater.

"Again?"

Bernie does a rapid scratching thing on her cheek that doesn't seem to correspond to a believable itch. "I won't bother with glasses." She leaps up and heads for the kitchen.

"Come on, Martha. I'll make you earrings with little stars. Tasteful." Leanne leans over to grab a pen off the end table and waves it.

I'm the last sixteen-year-old on the planet still whole about the ears. I pull myself off the floor and stretch out on the couch so I can submit myself to more faux earrings. The upholstery rasps my shoulder.

"Bernie never goes out with us anymore," Leanne says. "What's up with her?"

"Don't ask me." They don't bother inviting me out anymore. Dad's curfew messes up everyone's evening.

Tammy Mills, Leanne's friend—and mine by default—shows up in the doorway to the living room. She looks like a clone of Leanne with the same blonde waves, but with longer legs, good for keeping up. "I let myself in. Can I get a ride with you to town?" she asks Leanne.

"I'm leaving soon." Leanne waits tables at the Sunset Diner in Thorndale, a twenty minute drive from Putnam. She cranks my head to a better angle and presses the pen nib into my earlobe.

Bernie returns with an armful of pop cans. "You could try my old clip-ons," she says to me. "They're comfy. I'll find them." She leaves again to hurry upstairs. I'm not sure what's wrong with Bernie today. Nervous or something.

"Have you even considered getting your ears pierced?" Tammy Mills asks, although it's hard to hear with my head squished against the cushion.

"Of course. It's my dad with the problem. Not me, remember?"

"What's his problem, exactly?" Tammy Mills says.

Leanne's pressure on my ear eases. "He thinks it's mutilating the body."

"Doesn't think it projects a positive image," I add.

Bernie returns with earrings in the palm of her hand. The twin nests of beads are red and godawful. I tried screw-ons when I was nine, the kind with the c-clamps you crank on from the back, but they sent rivers of pain along the sides of my head.

I sit up and snap Bernie's eroded clasp against a lobe. She's right. They do feel okay.

"Look at you, Martha. *Tres chic*," Leanne says with a smirk.

"My great-grandma has a pair like that, only they're blue," says Tammy Mills.

I ignore her and hold my head carefully as I revel in the metallic sensation on my ears. Ornamenting one's body is an important form of artistic expression, I decide, and remember Velvet's hand-painted jeans.

"You could wear earrings like that for the 'something old' part at your wedding," Tammy Mills adds.

"John'll love them." Leanne tosses the pen aside and reaches for the TV *Guide*.

"I'm not sure I'll marry him," I say.

"Why not?" asks Tammy Mills, on the floor and checking the labels on Bernie's new sweaters. "He's not so bad."

"He's in the *audiovisual* club." Leanne has also commented on John's jeans, better suited to the '8o's, and his hair, parted in the middle and fanning out in little arcs.

"He's sweet and everything," I say.

"But what?" Tammy Mills holds up a fleecy pink V-neck.

"We're interested in different things."

Tammy's forehead screws up and she stares at me over the pinkness.

"Like art and stuff," I explain.

Leanne lowers the TV *Guide*. Bernie smiles at me. I wish I'd kept my big mouth shut. Dreams really are like cucumber blossoms. Highly delicate and embarrassingly loud in colour.

Tammy Mills folds up the sweater. "I like art. Mom just finished gluing a photograph of a duck on Dad's old rotary saw blade. It looks real nice. But I never saw an ad in the classfieds for 'artist wanted.'"

Leanne flips a crop of hair behind her shoulder. "Some people do take art at college."

I bet Velvet went to college.

"Although Martha's Dad might not be so keen," Leanne adds. "Especially when he finds out you draw," she passes us individual smiles, "naked people."

Weird. But interesting. Like Velvet herself.

"No!" Bernie says.

"Totally naked?" Tammy Mills's eyes go round. "That's illegal."

Leanne shrugs. "Not if everyone's a consenting adult. But first you have to get accepted into college before you can do any of the fun stuff." She swings her legs up under her and yawns. "Apparently getting in is next to impossible."

Bernie's earrings clench my earlobes, sending twin pains up my head worse than any screw-ons.

"Come on," Tammy Mills says.

"It's true," Leanne says. "Not that you need grades. But you know Lorna from the diner. Her cousin goes to college in Toronto and had to show the school a stack of something like twenty amazing, framed paintings. She spent a decade making them."

"Whoa," Tammy Mills says, exhaling slowly.

"Twenty paintings?" I remember the swirls on my pencil case and the smudged pencil drawings in my desk, and sink deeper into the couch.

"Maybe not twenty," Leanne says, "but lots. Even with the amazing paintings she would have been rejected. Luckily her uncle, some top honcho at the college, forced the department to accept her."

"That's awful," Bernie says.

"Good thing you've got John," Tammy Mills says to me. "They're rich over there. You wouldn't even have to work." She looks pleased with herself for arranging my future.

Bernie tilts her head. "Or there's always Lowe's Pickles."

"People become artists somehow," I say. "A girl is painting a sign for Norm." Suddenly, one of Bernie's earrings falls off my lobe, skips off the sofa and clunks on the floor. "Clip-ons are useless. Sorry, Bernie."

"We just use the peel-and-stick letters at our place," says Tammy Mills. "They never even wash off."

I swipe the earring off the floor and toss them both on the coffee table. "I'm going to the bathroom to find out what the hell Leanne did to my ears. Then I'm going home."

"Don't leave without thanking me," Leanne says.

I check myself in Bernie's bathroom mirror. Leanne didn't make stars after all. She left only mini ballpoint blue crosses, Christian types, one on each earlobe. Very funny. If I hold my head at an angle, they turn into x's. X marks the spots where I'll get these damn lobes pierced. I'll be painting by then too. So lost inside a storm of colour I won't have time to stop for anything, except maybe to nibble a dill pickle grown by some sorry farmer back in Putnam.

Chapter 6

A DAY LATER, I brake at the edge of Velvet's driveway and rewrap the orange flowers in my front basket. I wanted to bring her a gift. A sketchbook maybe, or a hammer to bang out the dent in her truck. All I could come up with was a handful of cucumber blossoms wrapped in wet toilet paper, but she'll sense my goodwill in the offering.

I stand astride my bike before the address of Velvet Rudder of Binscarth. The village is five miles west of Putnam in the opposite direction of Thorndale's town lights. Like Putnam, Velvet's village is another blink-and-you'll-miss-it kind of place. The kind Thorndale kids laugh at. Kids that can't see past rusted car parts from the junk dealer next door or the auto body repair across the highway. Velvet's place is like a pinball machine that was accidentally delivered to a funeral home. Her squat bungalow, set close to the road, is small and striped in dirty aluminum siding, but her mailbox is painted as a lion's head, cartoon yellow with a jaw that opens and shuts to eat the mail. A giant, wavy arrow points to her front doorbell.

I walk my bike past her truck and avoid looking at the dent in the door. I lean the bike against a chipped cement box planted with gigantic wooden lollipops. The afternoon heat is thick and the air is tinged with the smell of turpentine from the carport, where Velvet herself is wielding a paint roller. She's hunched over a sign. Quietly, so as not to disturb her, I float into the cool shadows. Vines made from green pipe cleaners twine up the rusted iron posts that support the carport roof. I stare and bump into a table.

Velvet shrieks. "When did you get here?"

"Just now."

"Jesus Murphy."

"You said to come by."

"Nothing like 'hello' to announce one's presence." She lowers her eyes to her work, but I can still see the snarl in them.

"Sorry," I say—a simple word to smooth life's bumps. I hope.

Velvet spins her paint roller along a wooden panel as long as a church pew and stretched across two sawhorses. As she rolls out a swath of creamy white, my regular-sized desire for painting cranks up to a heart-banging ache. I reach for a tin can on the table, blooming with paintbrushes. I finger a thick handle poking out from a bouquet of spattered tools.

She looks up. Coughs.

I jam my hands in my pockets. A fly buzzes into the carport, falls silent and zooms away, as uninterested in my visit as Velvet. As the hush lingers, I wonder if Velvet might not be as keen about accepting me into her art world as I'd hoped. "Anyway," I say, "nice to see your place and everything." I shrink back a few steps just to see what she'll do.

Velvet paints on. She doesn't look up.

I take one more slow motion step backward as she lowers her roller into the paint tray and works it back and forth.

If only my dad hadn't hyped me up with success talk. If only I hadn't assumed Velvet would sign on as my personal art guru.

I glare at the paintbrushes, turn and head for my bike. For a life empty of artistic inspiration.

"I suppose I could thank you for not smashing your bike into my garage upon arrival," Velvet calls out to the driveway, just as my fingers wrap around the handlebar.

I let the handlebar go, prance back into the carport and hope my high-beam smile doesn't blind her. "You're welcome!"

With the wood grain clouded in white, Velvet lays down her roller. She just needed to finish her job with full concentration, that's all. Relief floods me.

"Your place is amazing," I say. "Did you decorate it yourself?"

"Indeed. Welcome to my castle." She dips her head for a regal bow. "Well, rented castle."

I move closer to the whitewashed plywood. "Is that sign for the Schellenbergers?"

"No. Norm's job is still under advisement. Mine, that is. Maybe yours, too. You know the guy better than I do."

She does want my company. My *advisement*. I spin a vinyl topped stool in my direction and plop down at a paint-splattered table.

"Have a look at my Schellenberger design." Velvet saunters to the table I'm leaning across and flips open a binder. It's stuffed with drawings penned on napkins, envelope backs and grocery receipts. Good thing I didn't get her a lame sketchbook. Sketchbooks must be for stuck up, over-privileged artists—not raw, intense ones like Velvet. I wrap my feet around the stool legs and crane over her binder as she perches on the stool across from me. She pulls out a sheet covered in a fit of pencil marks.

Norm's design is egg-shaped and cracked open at the top with a rooster surging out and announcing the name of the farm. Shafts of morning sunlight radiate from behind the rooster's head. I stroke his penciled tail feathers. "Your drawing is so layered." I bet Velvet doesn't even own an eraser. She just piles lines on top of one another, each level growing darker, fiercer and louder than the one before. "How did your brain turn out an idea like that?"

"Norm Schellenberger," Velvet says, pointing to his lettering with a grimy fingernail. "He's a yeller, is he not?"

"A yeller?"

"A blustering kind of guy with too much to do and too much to say about it. Like a rooster in the morning. Friendly enough. He'd give you the coveralls off his bod, but he can't stop shouting orders."

"It's true." Velvet gets people, even when she hardly knows them. "That's Norm exactly."

Velvet rotates the binder for a better view. "I consider this concept as a portrait-in-letters. One of my more progressive ideas. One the Binscarth-Putnam crowd might not be ready for, Norm Schellenberger included." Suddenly, her eyes narrow. "The problem is, Maria—"

"Martha." I swallow.

"Right. The problem is, I'm tired of painting drop-dead boring Roman letters on white ground." Velvet's top lip curls up. "If I have to paint one more silhouette of a goddamn cow, I'll shoot myself, I swear." She bangs the binder shut.

"No, Velvet." I lunge for her book. "You can't."

"This job," she says, holding up a trembling index finger and whispering ferociously, "is sucking the life out of me."

I stifle a gasp. "How? You've got it all. Freedom. Paint. Your own studio."

"Don't you understand? People around here are killing me, sign by sign."

"But I thought signs told truths. Expressed portraits in letters." How in hell can she help me if she gives up?

"They *could* tell truths," Velvet says, "if anyone would let them. But name one person willing to look at an honest portrayal of himself. One soul on this godforsaken earth who will confess to her true being, bloody and miserable as it is, or jealous or fearful or clumsy or lazy. No one wants to sit for that portrait, Martha. Not when there's an alternative. Not when they can choose a safe, tidy version," her fists ball up, "in a *Roman font.*"

It's like I was biking full speed ahead to my golden destination and someone knocked me into the ditch. Dazed, I stare at the cement floor. "My dad wouldn't sit for an honest portrait." My voice feels thick and slow. "Or my mother. Or my sister, come to think of it, or Bernie. No one is willing." No one in greater Putnam can help me become an artist, either. I need someone. I needed Velvet. She could have been the one to guide me in making a gigantic stack of paintings for art college. But she's too miserable to help herself. I slump back in my stool.

"Are you willing?" Velvet's voice slices into me.

"What? To be honest?"

"Yes."

"Sure. I guess," I say, my voice shaky.

"Wait." Velvet leans in so close inside my personal space I can feel her musty breath. "Don't blurt out an answer without considering my question carefully. Quiet your mind, Martha." She floats her hands into stillness, like a choir director closing the hymn. "Ask yourself. Are you truly committed to artistic honesty?"

"Yes," my mouth says, which is a lie, really, since I have no idea what she's talking about.

"Good." Velvet presses toward me, her closeness as uncomfortable as an itchy wool sweater. Finally, she leans back. "You're not completely sure, but you're willing to try. Here's your first assignment. Listen carefully."

Hope for her guidance comes racing home with a spine-tingle of possibility.

She climbs off her stool, stands tall and peers toward an invisible thinking spot in the rafters of the carport. "Paint a truth," she says. "On my truck. Close to the spot where you rammed into it."

I stare at her. Scratch my head. "I don't get it."

Velvet doesn't have that Mount Vesuvius look like she did a few minutes ago, when she was erupting about the evils of sign painting. Her finger isn't shaking and jabbing the air anymore. She's just standing calmly, arms folded in front of her. "Do you remember running into my truck?"

I feel my cheeks go hot. "Yes."

"Do you remember how you felt when your bicycle tire struck?" A twitch in her forehead gathers force. "The sound of impact? The transformation of a pristine expanse of red door into a buckled, tortuous horror?" She seems to hold back a growl clawing to escape.

"I remember." The heat surges up my face. Velvet has no friendly guidance to share. She just wants me to pay.

"Or maybe your memories are different," she says, returning to an almost kindly tone. "Whatever you decide to emphasize, paint a truthful response to the collision. An image, a phrase, a poem, an object. Whatever you like."

I fold my arms over my chest. "A truth?"

"A truth."

What the hell? "Why don't I just give you cash? I'll get a cheque from Lowe's next week."

She gazes out the carport, past her neighbour's garage to the cornfields in the distance. "Keep your money, Martha. Honesty in art is our greatest reward."

"Couldn't we start with something easier?"

A Cruella de Vil glare darkens Velvet's eyes. "Art is never easy." She pivots on her spattered Converse running shoe toward a jumble of paint tins on a shelf. "You have my array of One Shot paint at your disposal. Excellent for lettering signs, interior or exterior. Can I assume you have your own brushes?"

I kick at the table leg. "There's an old one in the toolbox at home. It's probably crusty." Doesn't she have anything fun and simple to paint? *Honey For Sale*? I'd take a sign for an earthworm farm over the truck painting.

Velvet shakes her head in disgust. She rifles through her brushes, plucks out a slim one and sets it on the table in front of me.

I stare at the brush. A mean-spirited revenge painting is all she wants. I owe her for ramming into her stupid truck, which I'm more sorry for than ever. I'll make her a painting. I pay my debts, but I won't be hanging out with Velvet Rudder and talking shop. I climb off the stool, my legs unsteady under the force of her eyes, and stumble out from her carport shadows and the stench of turpentine.

"Don't forget the brush," she calls. "Its size will affect your design."

I return to snap up the paintbrush off the table, and leave again with the brush clamped in my fist. Velvet doesn't bother saying goodbye. Neither do I.

The wilted cucumber blossoms are sagging in my front basket. I'm glad I forgot to give them to her. As soon as I hit the road, I toss the grubby orange mess into the ditch.

LATE THAT NIGHT, I creep downstairs to hunt for sketching paper. I can't sleep. If I can somehow make a stupid truck design, I'll be able to get the sign painter out of my mind. Rest. Move on. Let go of half-baked artist dreams. Resolve to appreciate John more.

By the skimpy moonlight slanting in through the window, I pull scrap paper from the altar in the dining room. The sheets are torn into jagged, clumsy halves, but who cares? I'll just get the design over with. I'm returning to my choir loft when Dad lumbers out from his bedroom. I curse silently. Positive thinking isn't on my agenda.

I make the bottom stair when he whisper-yells, "Martha! Can't sleep either?"

"I need to write down a few things," I call through the dim light. "Then I'm going back to bed."

"Sit down with me!" I hear Dad sliding a bowl from the kitchen cupboard. Two bowls. "Cereal?"

"I'm not hungry."

"I need an update on your sign painting. I can't wait another minute!" Dad tries setting the bowls on the communion table gently, but they clatter on the wood.

"Gerald?" Mom calls from the bedroom, her voice heavy with sleep.

"Go back to sleep, Peggy. Martha and I are having a little chat!"

I drop the papers on the steps and plod to the table as Dad pours himself an avalanche of Cheerios. He pauses, looks puzzled at the rectangle of cardboard missing from the side of the box, and sets it down. "Tell me how much Norm loved your design. Are you starting right away or does he need changes first?"

I wait for him to slosh milk on his mountain of cereal and pretend to be fascinated by its crackling noises. "I'm not painting Norm's sign." I cringe.

Dad looks bewildered. "Why not? I called ahead."

"I know," I moan.

He suspends his spoon in mid air. "I don't understand."

"Norm..." I fold my arms across my chest, "seems set with Velvet."

Dad frowns. "Did you even discuss the matter with him?"

I reach for a runaway Cheerio on the table and nibble it. "I'm not ready to paint signs."

"You didn't speak to him after I told him about your exceptional talent? Your determination to surpass the competition in design, quality and workmanship? I went the extra mile for you, Martha."

Avoiding eye contact is best.

"Oh, Martha. Martha, Martha. You *didn't* talk to Norm." Dad grasps tufts of hair on the sides of his head and shakes it mournfully. "I should have driven over and talked to him in person."

"Sorry, Dad." I crumple the plaid hem of my pajama top. "I couldn't."

"*Couldn't?* Can't? Won't?" Dad stands up and circles the table, waving his spoon in the air. "How many times do I have to tell you? Those words don't belong in a positive thinker's vocabulary!" He stops. "Now, Martha. Tell me what you've done to move yourself forward in your art career."

"I talked to the sign painter. I showed her my design."

"You talked to the competition?" Dad's spoon looks like it just keeled over and died.

"I was hoping she could help me."

"No, Martha. You can't expect help from your competitors." Dad articulates his syllables slowly to benefit the business-challenged. "Their mission is your failure."

"She didn't seem too keen on me," I admit.

Dad tosses down the spoon and claps his hands together like he's announcing a fresh start. "Here's how we'll move forward. You'll have nothing more to do with the competition. Understand? No communication." He pretend zips his lips shut.

My pleasure, I think, although I won't mention Velvet's stupid truth painting. It'll be over soon enough.

"And of course," Dad continues, "you'll excel through—"

"Positive affirmations," I say, but sound more like Eeyore on a bad day. "I know about them."

"Good! Then we just have to review them. Every night, ten minutes. Minimum. In a week we'll ramp up to fifteen. Work with the 'I'm a can-doer' phrase for now. The power to succeed comes from within, Martha."

A few years back, he thought the power came from God, but times change. "Corporate leaders pay me a handsome fee for that kind of advice," he continues. "I gave the same set of affirmations to Debbie, and she's responding beautifully. No more negative thinking." He mashes negativity into the pine floorboards with his slipper. "Agreed?"

"Sure, Dad." I fight off a yawn.

"And when you've absorbed the affirmations, *I'll* hire you to paint a sign. How does that sound?"

Oh, God. "You don't have to."

"Uh-uh." Dad holds up a hand. "I heard a 'don't.'"

"But I have to find my own style. You'll want me to paint mammoth positive affirmations or something."

"Martha." Dad's eyes gleam. "You're on to something."

I stand up and silently pray that our conversation will turn into a forgotten nightmare by morning. As Dad bids me a positively enriching sleep, I clomp upstairs, too exhausted by his energy to design Velvet's stupid truck painting. Dad's affirmations sound as false and empty as a plastic cucumber, but he's right about one thing: I'm as good as done with Velvet Rudder.

Chapter 7

THE NEXT DAY, Tammy Mills and I hitch a ride with Leanne to Thorndale. The town is home to our high school, a sign with a four-figure population count, and two stoplights with a string of stores in between them, including the Sunset Diner. A Tim Hortons landed in Thorndale last year, but so far we're holding out at the diner, at least while Leanne still works there.

Leanne scores us a seat with banana yellow vinyl seats that reach up past our heads. "Earth to Martha. I said, 'what are you having?'"

Our waitress is tapping a pen against her skirt and waiting.

I drag my attention to the waitress. "Oh. Diet Sprite." I can't stop wondering what to do for Velvet's truck. I could paint a hand grenade-sized rock inside the dent, but that wouldn't be owning up to my part of the crash.

"Get a large. It's free." Leanne winks at the waitress.

"Free? That's great." Tammy Mills says as the waitress leaves.

"We're glad you could come out." Leanne smiles at me too warmly. "Even if it's just for a pop. You've been working too much."

"Way too much." Tammy Mills shakes her head sadly.

"Your hands must be raw from all that picking," adds Leanne.

I cross my arms. "What do you guys want from me?"

"Nothing!" Leanne says. "How's the cucumber harvest anyway?"

"Better than—"

"How are things with Bernie?" Tammy Mills moves her cutlery in closer to mine, and fiddles with the corner of a sugar packet. In a lower voice, she says, "Leanne and me think she's been acting weird."

"Weird how?" I swear the two of them dredge up scandal for entertainment.

"She never comes out with us anymore," Leanne says.

"She hasn't been to any parties lately," Tammy Mills adds.

"I haven't been out much either." I shimmy in my seat, away from Tammy Mills.

"Your dad never lets you. That's normal for you," Tammy Mills says as the waitress sets down our drinks.

"You're awesome, Lorna," Leanne tells her.

"I do so come out," I say. "I went to the bar with you."

"Once. Your dad was at some seminar thing. Doesn't matter," Leanne says. "I wonder if Bernie is pissed because of what I said the other day when we were looking at her sweaters."

"About her ship coming in," Tammy adds. "And laughing, like it'd never happen."

"Do you think she was hurt?" Leanne asks, and the two of them look at me with moon eyes—almost convincing renditions of concern.

"I don't think she cares what you say," I lie.

"I wonder." As Leanne reaches above her head in a deliciously long cat-stretch, her mouth slithers into a thin smile. "Maybe Bernie was blushing that day because her ship really has come in."

"Huh?" I say.

"Maybe," Leanne lets her arms down slowly and drops her voice to a whisper, "Bernie has a secret lover."

"Very funny." I jab my straw at an ice cube and hope a truck painting idea will reveal itself within the glass, like a subliminal message you just have to hunt for. "Martha," Leanne says, suddenly grave. "I guess Bernie didn't tell you. Tammy and I saw her the other night at two in the morning."

"So?"

"She was walking the street in Putnam."

"Bernie never told me anything." They're making up stories.

"She looked like she just stepped out of a clothes dryer." Leanne tosses her locks and leans in. "Her hair was squashed flat on one side and poking out on the other, and her shirt was mashed up at the front." One of Leanne's crescent-shaped eyebrows arches up. "Like she'd just had a roll in the hay," her other eyebrow dips lower, "and was on her way home."

I shove my drink away and shake my head. "Bernie. With a guy. In Putnam. Trust me. I pick with her almost every morning. She would have told me."

"You've been with her too much," Leanne says. "You don't see the change. It's hard on us."

"Me and Leanne don't feel right asking her to buy vodka anymore," Tammy Mills says. "If Bernie's not partying with us, it's hard to ask. Last time she couldn't find the Smirnoff and bought the expensive stuff, but we were okay with that."

"So this is all about vodka?"

"No. We're concerned about Bernie," Leanne says.

"You just want dirt," I say.

"And maybe a little vodka," Tammy Mills says.

"Everything is better with vodka," Leanne adds, trading smiles with Tammy Mills. Then her smile fades. "We have no one to buy for us. You don't understand what a difficult position that puts us in at parties."

"Did Bernie seem upset that night?" I ask.

"She was fine," Leanne says impatiently. "Ask her if she has anyone special in her life, okay? We feel like we're losing her. Will you see her tomorrow? Or are you off to the sign painter's place?"

My neck stiffens. "How did you know I went there?"

"I forget who saw you biking there." Leanne glances at Tammy Mills, who shrugs.

"The Schellenbergers are having a sign painted," I say. "I biked over to help pick out colours." So much for honesty in art.

"Seriously?" says Tammy Mills. "I heard that Velvet girl is crazy."

"You heard right," I say.

"She flips out if you don't like her signs," Tammy Mills says. "My mom told me. Velvet made one for the neighbours. It had glow-in-the-dark colours and a mechanical corn stalk that sprouted a cob in the mornings and shrank back behind the sign at night."

I could admire the sign idea, but I won't.

"Oh, my." With her pinkie extended, Leanne dabs the corners of her mouth with a napkin. "A sign with a hard-on."

"The Elliotts complained the sign wasn't what they agreed to," Tammy Mills continues, "so that Velvet girl carted it away and got it chewed up into wood chips. Dumped them on the family's flower garden. Then she made them a regular sign with normal letters."

I was thinking of painting a simple apology on Velvet's truck, but I have a feeling nothing will satisfy her. "I'm only going to her place one more time."

"She'd be legal," Tammy Mills says. "Could you ask her to buy us vodka?"

I snort. "I don't want to deal with her any more than I have to."

"Then talk to Bernie," Leanne says. "Start by finding out if she's seeing someone."

I roll my eyes. "Believe me, Bernie Schellenberger is single. Unattached. On her own. She was probably overtired from picking cucumbers the other night and wandered around in her sleep."

I slurp to the bottom of my Diet Sprite. I have to get out of here and put to rest an apprenticeship with a sign painter.

THE FOLLOWING DAY, John and I visit my sister's place, a country mile from Putnam. Doreen wants me to check out a dresser she doesn't need.

Along the way, a grin floats on John's lips, but his mood doesn't lighten my side of the car. I stare out the side window and watch the cornfields and fence lines swoosh by. I thought I had a chance with Velvet. Now all I've got left are my vodka-obsessed friends and John, glowing with a strangely vibrant happiness. Maybe the aliens got to him.

My sister Doreen is Mennonite-by-choice. Don't blame my side of the family. It was her husband Leonard's fault, although Doreen has always been tight with the Lord Jesus. Maybe she had an in when our dad was a minister, so Leonard, a black car Menno, figured she'd do. After they got married, Doreen got more Mennonite than Leonard. I guess she had to show the community she was up for the job. Or maybe she was striving to be her Mennonite best, like Dad does with his business.

In ankle-length, mud-stained dresses, her two girls run barefoot down the laneway to greet us.

"Brought you something," I say to the girls. Mary is five and Anna, seven. I slip two long cucumbers from my backpack and hold them up like juggling pins. "Magic wands. Make a wish."

Mary lunges for hers, giggling, but Anna scowls. Wands are too demonic or something. Her parents wouldn't approve of magic, but a cucumber would be appreciated.

"Actually, they're clubs," John says. "Careful!" He takes the cukes from me, faux-bonks the girls on the head, and then hands them each a vegetable.

"You're funny," says Mary, squinting up at John. Funny is different.

The Friday before my sister married Leonard, I kept my tears pressed down all through school and the bus ride home. By then my throat burned from holding in the hurt, although I wasn't so much sad as angry. Doreen was leaving me; the only offspring left for Dad to lord over on a daily basis.

Doreen, on the porch, prompts the girls. "Thank you, Martha." She's got the whole Menno get-up: the rumpled navy dress and gauzy white prayer cap. A black car sits on the gravel laneway. Her fingers, raspberry red, pinch the sides of empty quart baskets.

"Thank you, Martha," the girls say in unison. Mary prances on the spot, and Anna stares at the triangle of flesh my neckline traces. Anna wouldn't think of me as a slut but she knows about your generic sinner. And I wore pants in this heat just for them. They'd have preferred a skirt, but please.

Doreen holds out baskets to the girls. "Fill one more each. The ripe ones are at the far end." As they dance off to the raspberry rows, she jabs her head toward the front door. "I want to show you two the dresser."

We follow her inside, up the wooden stairs to her second floor, stripped bare of the rose carpet. Doreen and Leonard are getting rid of wedding presents. The blender, the toaster oven and anything else with an electrical cord are gone. So are luxuries like good china and the floral throw rug.

"The oak dresser," she reminds us.

"What's wrong with it?" John asks.

"It has a mirror."

When we reach the bedroom, I run my hands over the top of the dresser, dusty and empty of the framed wedding pictures. It's like she's passing on an inheritance, only she's still alive. It's her modern life in the twentieth century that passed away.

"What's wrong with mirrors anyway?" I ask.

"Mirrors are ... well, they're for vanity." Doreen stands tall beside the hulking chest of drawers. The wall behind is bare and white, and the heat up here as dense and heavy as the block quilt on the bed.

I help myself to a tattered paperback, *Mennonites and Discipleship*, off the top of the dresser, and fan it in front of my face. Scrawny, useless thing. I wave harder, but it doesn't help. "I already have a dresser, Doreen. What am I going to do with another one?"

"If you like, we could store it for you. Until your family grows." Doreen might be hiding a smile.

"It's bigger than I thought." The top of the dresser is at eye level. "Bulky, too. I just can't think about furniture-of-the-future now. You'll have to find someone else, Doreen."

John runs his hand along the side of the dresser. "You sure you want to sell this? You could lop off the mirror and keep it."

"You can't amputate a piece of furniture," I say. Some people have no respect for design.

"She's right." Doreen tucks a lock into her gauzy cap. "It'd destroy the value. Why don't you take the dresser, John? I wouldn't accept more than a hundred. You know new dressers aren't made as well, don't you? The drawers fall apart, but one like this will last a lifetime." She raps on the oak top. If Doreen doesn't finalize her career as a Mennonite, she could sell used cars off the lot in town. "Besides, I'd like to keep this dresser in the family. Not that you're family, John. Not yet, anyway," she adds, practically pinning his leaf to the family tree.

I toss the book, useless as a fan, back on the dresser.

"I've got boxes of household things to give away in the shed, too," Doreen adds.

"I'll go through them," John says. "I'll be setting up house sometime." He slings an arm around me. "Martha is moving in with me when she's done school, Doreen. Did I tell you?"

"Since when?" I shrug off his arm. "You'll be long gone to university by then."

"After you get married?" Doreen's eyes sparkle. "Oh, Martha!" Mennonites aren't partial to excessive hugging, but I can feel one aching to bust out of Doreen.

I step back, just in case. "Nothing is finalized."

"Don't be embarrassed, Martha." Doreen's cheeks ball up into joyful, pink cherries. "I am so happy for you."

"Slow down, Doreen." Strange thing to say to a Mennonite.

"Oh, no rush," she says, beaming. "No rush at all." She smoothes her apron and turns to John. "There's good land up in Ridley township. More affordable, too. Have you been up there?"

"Several times," John says. "A hundred acre lot is for sale on the seventh line. It's got a decent barn and a solid brick house. Three bedrooms."

Doreen gazes at me in awe. "A brick house, Martha."

"It's not like he's bought anything." I avoid meeting her eyes and rub the heel of my hand, sore from cucumber prickles.

"Martha!" Doreen claps her hands together like she's just remembered something important, turns and sits on the bed with a swoosh of her skirts. "Here's something you'll have no trouble storing." She slides open the drawer of her nightstand and pulls out a small, velvet-covered box. It squeaks when she lifts the lid.

My heart does a hiccup.

A trio of gold rings is scattered on a miniature satin pillow: her diamond solitaire and their two wedding bands. "Take these, why don't you," she says, like they're extra sweaters she outgrew.

"You're giving away your *wedding rings*?" I look in Doreen's eyes for a window to her sadness.

"Take them." She snaps the lid shut and shakes it and the rings rattle.

"Too fancy?"

"Much." Her eyes are clear and her voice as matter-of-fact as her life.

"You don't want to save them for the girls?" John asks.

"No rings are worn at all." She takes my hand and sets the box on my palm.

John moves in, opens the lid and peeks inside. "There's an engagement ring."

Doreen glows like a Christmas tree, the mammoth one they park outside Thorndale Town Hall. "The complete package."

The blue softness of the velvet nestles into my hand, but Doreen and Leonard's rings don't belong to me. I clamp the lid shut. "I can't take the rings either." Something is wrong with a world where a girl gets wedding rings before she can get her ears pierced.

"Just take them, Martha. At least I'll know they're safe."

I attend to a splinter of cucumber prickle, all chewed apart. Seems to be part of my hand now, but the more I touch it, the more the pain bites in.

"That's incredibly generous of you, Doreen," John says, his gaze still fixed on the box.

"Martha marrying and staying close to home is for my benefit, too. I'm a loss to Mom, living the way we do. And with all Dad's wild business ideas that never seem to go anywhere," Doreen adds, "let's just say Mom is fortunate to have someone steady like Martha."

The front screen door bangs shut downstairs, and Leonard bounds up the steps.

"I'm not that steady," I say.

"Have we got a new home for the dresser?" Leonard appears in the doorway. He's growing his hair into a blunt, cropped length. A chin-bordered beard is sprouting up too.

"I thought a hundred dollars would be fair," Doreen tells him. "For family. *Near family.*" She catches Leonard's eye and holds it.

My stomach twists up.

"Family?" Leonard smiles until his forehead glows. "For family, the dresser is free."

John backs up a step.

"I'd be glad to give away the dresser." Doreen's cheeks ball up again. "We're not putting too much pressure on you, are we, Martha?"

I want to tell them all that I'm not ready to make marriage decisions, but the weight of Doreen, Leonard, John and the big oak dresser keeps me silent. John rests a hand on the dresser. Everyone looks at me and waits.

"John will get good use out of the dresser," I finally say, and realize that letting him in on the family heirlooms doesn't feel so bad.

John slings his arm around me. Doreen demonstrates the dresser's deep drawers, big enough for a couple's things. Leonard smiles at me and then at John, like he's recognized us for the first time as newly minted adults. As future husband and wife. I slip the velvet box into my back pocket. It's not like I have a place in the art world. My shoulders fall, and I let myself sink under the pressure of John's arm.

Chapter 8

THE NEXT DAY, I return to Velvet's place to complete my extremely short sign painting apprenticeship. The more I think about it, the more John and I make sense. Maybe even living on a farm someday, and growing cucumbers there. This morning, Bernie and I picked and picked until the burlap bags were bursting. I know what I'm good at, and I'm not ashamed to say that it's growing vegetables.

With Velvet's paintbrush jammed in the back pocket of my cut-offs, I stand at the entrance to her carport and clear my throat. Velvet is hunched over the same white sign, pulling navy paint along a foot-high letter for a horse farm. My heart jumps at the parade of penciled letters unfolding across the panel and waiting to be born in colour, but I squash down hopes for bringing them to life. "Excuse me."

"Hmm," Velvet murmurs and continues painting.

"I'm here to paint your truck. Doesn't matter what colour." I cross my arms and tap the toe of my sandal impatiently. "Whatever you've got lots of."

Velvet shifts on her stool and dips her brush into the paint can.

Apparently, I'm invisible. "I'll just grab something." I march to her supply shelf and read the titles on small tins of paint. Slide out a can of orange that doesn't look too goopy around the lid.

"Take the yellow," she says. "There isn't much call for it."

I keep my grumbling low and exchange the orange for a can of a pissy hue and dredge up a screwdriver from a heap of tools on the table, which takes about a year given Velvet's lack of interest in helping.

"What sort of design did you have in mind?" Velvet finally asks.

"Nothing much. Some tendrils. Little shoots of foliage from lilies. Those flowers people bring to funerals." It's a stupid idea, but it'll be over with soon. I pry open the lid. "I was going to swirl them around the dent."

Velvet sets her brush down and stands up. "Flowers for a funeral?"

I shrug and wipe a wayward blotch of yellow from my cut-offs, but more colour bleeds into the denim.

"Who died? Or should I say, what died?" Velvet seems to be checking the rafters. I'm not sure I should answer her.

I pick out a flat stick from the pile of tools and swirl the yellow.

"Was that your only idea?" she asks.

"It's not good enough?"

"I'm curious."

I sigh and mention the faux rock painting, the lettered apology, and the idea I had on the bike ride here about advertising her neighbour's auto body repair shop on her truck.

"I like the tendril concept. I agree. It's the best one." Velvet starts pacing the cement floor. "Funereal flowers. I can picture them splayed out from the dent. A hushed reminder of a life lived, but lost. And yet, a bud of hope for new beginning."

"I'll get it over with." I lay the stir stick down.

Velvet marches up to me and takes hold of the paint can. "Don't get the painting over with."

"But I want to go home." I grip the can.

"It's not necessary to actually paint the design."

"I said I'd do the truck assignment, and I will." I squeeze the can tighter, but when Velvet pulls it away from me, a yellow tidal wave sloshes over the rim and glops onto her floor.

Patiently, she removes a blotchy cloth off the supply table and bends down to mop yellow from the floor. "My neighbour at the auto body repair shop fixed the door already. He owed me for painting his front door."

So her stupid truck is fixed. I dig my fingernail into my palms. Like I have nothing better to do than envision signs that'll never exist. Or gaze longingly at Lytton Stables lettering awaiting high gloss navy from an opened can. "Then my assignment is over." I pull her brush from my pocket and ram it into the coffee can.

Velvet repositions the brush. "Martha. Relax. Take a seat on my stool and lean against the wall."

I plunk down on her stool, a kind thing to do for my legs, which are exhausted from squatting over too many cucumber plants.

"That's it," she says. "Just watch you don't knock over the paint can."

I survey the horse sign before me.

"Norm Schellenberger," Velvet says, "as you probably know, hated the rooster idea. Hated the cracked egg and the bird shouting the name of his farm." A bitter edge creeps into her voice. "The design was a flop."

"I didn't know." On the table, Velvet's pencilled lettering gallops across the expanse of white. I breathe in the piercing scent of potential floating from her paint tin.

"He said the rooster made him look like Foghorn Leghorn." Velvet lowers herself on a splattered chair. "He laughed in my face."

"Oh. I'm sorry."

"*You're* sorry." Her shoulders slump. "I spent hours coming up with that idea." She cups her face in her hands and rubs her temples. "The man has no vision."

"More chickenshit than rooster," I offer. I run a finger down the satiny shaft of paintbrush stretched across the lid of the paint can. I slow to a stop at the silver collar embracing the bristles. Their navy tips glisten.

"He's a chicken all right," Velvet says.

"Even skitters around like one."

"This way, that way." Velvet sways her shoulders and even smiles.

"Although he's letting Bernie and me use his land." I lift the brush off the lid and hold it up like an extension of my index finger. "I should watch what I say."

"And he's paying me good money to letter his sign," Velvet agrees.

I dip the brush nestled between my fingertips into the navy paint and swirl circles in the gleaming pool. "What about painting chicken footprints for Norm?"

Velvet's shoulders perk up. "That's an interesting idea."

I lift the brush and watch a droplet of blue clutch the bristles and finally fall into the pond below. I lower the brush onto the wood, between the penciled edges of a letter. Trail a glistening sheen, thick as nail polish and just as pungent.

"The sign could have one big chicken footprint." Thrill pulses in Velvet's voice. "Set like an arrow pointing to the Schellenberger name." She glances at my painted letter. "Stay tight in the lines. Horse farmers are snooty. Everything has to be more perfect than usual."

My knuckles tense. The brush stands stiff at attention. Caught with my hand in the paint can. But Velvet doesn't seem to mind. My fingers relax. I pause to consider Norm's design. "What if you dipped a chicken's feet in that yellow you don't need, and let the bird hop all over his sign?"

"Yes!" Velvet's eyes glisten. "A Jackson Pollockesque, random spattering of chicken-like essence!"

Whatever that means. I brush on the rest of the navy letter, start into the next one and imagine a glorious possibility: Velvet blabbing incoherently in the distance for days on end while I independently finish the horse sign. And the next one and the one after that, until a gigantic stack of paintings grows on the cement floor. Paintings to show art colleges, one of which takes me on, nurtures me and grants me passage out of Putnam, Ontario and onto bigger, better, art-loving worlds beyond.

John's shadow lurks in the corner of my mind, but I push it away.

"Let's do it!" Velvet cries.

I hold the brush high. "Really?" I remember Norm's sign and lower the brush. "But shouldn't we get Norm to approve the design?"

"To hell with approval. When inspiration strikes, an artist must harness its energy."

"Makes sense." I sit back to assess my still wet painting. If I had a camera, I'd take a picture of my two letters and carry them in my wallet forever and ever.

"It makes *no* sense, Martha. No sense at all! But it's brilliant. A truthful yet subtle comment on Norm's sensibility—not that he needs to know—that keeps pace with the experimentation so prevalent in contemporary art. Paint, Martha. Paint like hell! Finish the horse sign." Velvet plucks from her tools a pair of purple goggles, more beach worthy than for safety, and strides to the table saw. She shoves the goggles on and powers up the table saw, off and on again like a motorcycle driver revving an engine. "I'll cut the wood," she yells over the motor. "Stay back!"

"How am I supposed to paint these letters anyway?" I yell.

"Any way that works!" she yells back.

"Velvet?"

"What?"

"How do you get your hair to stick up like that?"

"Elmer's glue!" she yells.

Velvet Rudder even has art supplies for her hair. God, I love this place.

Velvet heaves a massive sheet of plywood onto her table saw and drives it through, sending a spray of sawdust arcing into the air and fluttering down like a magical, glittering snowfall. She shuts off the table saw and slides the goggles onto the top of her head. "Honesty to oneself is our top priority as artists," she says more calmly, "but there are bills to pay. That's when guys in agribusiness come in handy."

Agribusiness. John. My brush wobbles over the contour of a letter, but I paint on and bring the horse sign's faint letters into full coloured life.

Chapter 9

THAT WEEK, I return to Velvet's shop every afternoon. She teaches me what to do if you drop a paint blob somewhere unfortunate, and how to eat an apple whole, core and all, like she does. Apples and Frito Lay corn chips are her favourite paint shop snacks. "Apples bring back memories of my early youth," she explains. "Corn chips I love because I never got them in my youth." Except for that single comment, Velvet hasn't said a word about her life outside of sign painting. She's never asked me inside her house either. We're operating on a strictly professional basis.

Today, we're working on the Schellenberger sign, the one with the chicken footprints. From a neighbour, Velvet secures the use of a live bird who doesn't mind dipping its feet in yellow paint. The challenge is in encouraging the chicken to stay inside the edges of the sign. Eventually we fence her in and reward our feathered assistant with corn chips, even though her footprints are more fleeting and less pronounced than we would have liked.

Velvet and I are repainting the footprints more vividly. Lost in the dance of colour, I hardly think about John's plans for us to someday move to Ridley township.

"Are you sure we should be doing this?" I daub on extra paint. "All this touch up work isn't breaking our resolution about honesty in art, is it?"

"Art can't be appreciated if it isn't legible," Velvet says. "There are times when an artist must improve on the truth."

I lift up my brush to think. "Like when you use eyeliner."

"Exactly." Velvet even stops painting. "As soon as you told me about the idea of funeral flowers on my truck, I knew you had the mind of an artist. A bit of a shaky hand, but first steps are like that."

I set my brush on the lid of the can. "You don't think I load up my brush too much?" I ask to encourage the direction of her comments.

"You load your brush fine. Do me a favour, Martha. Grab me another paint cloth. I dripped."

Sixteen long years I've lived just to hear a person fawn over my efforts with a paintbrush, and already we've moved off topic.

"Check in that trunk under the table," she adds. "You'll find a pile of old cloths inside."

Still aglow from Velvet's comments regarding my artistic nature, I drift to her ancient trunk. It has two cracked leather straps you have to pry from their buckles. Doesn't help that the leather is more beef jerky than tenderloin. Finally, I creak open the lid. A mildew smell billows up and a dusty spider scurries out like he got caught going at it with the neighbour girl in the haymow. There's a pile of frayed dishtowels inside, stained brown like old lady liver spots.

Velvet is hunched over a footprint, so deep in concentration she's barely breathing, let alone noticing my trunk perusal.

I wonder. What does a lone sign painter with no discernable life outside work keep inside a trunk? As thankful as I am for the chance to apprentice under Velvet, it's strange how little I know about her.

I lift out the dishtowels. Underneath, I find a newspaper article from the *Toronto Star* that sends a tingle of excitement up my arms. *New Work by Velvet Rudder* is the headline and the name of her art show. I check the October date from four years ago and devour the article. Velvet, my teacher and guide, is famous. Her show featured "dark messages and the dichotomy between public and private thoughts in text-based imagery". She must be exceptionally talented. As the review's words sink into babble, I imagine Velvet swarmed with crowds and presented with armfuls of roses from appreciative fans. I read the final line: "Given Rudder's adolescent messages, perhaps she should have kept them private until she has matured."

Adolescent? I glance up at Velvet, still painting, and read on.

"Her efforts at mimicking a professional sign painter's craftsmanship fall well short of the mark."

So maybe she didn't get many bouquets.

I lay the newspaper article down quietly, but Velvet's head snaps to attention and her brush clatters to the floor. She marches over to me, still squatting before her trunk of crap. "Keep your fingers where they belong," she hisses in her best vice-principal voice.

I yank my hand back as she slams down the lid. In silent shock, I stare at my spared appendage. Velvet could have cracked my fingers off.

"I don't need One Shot paint smudging up all my things and your hands are a mess. As usual." She looks at me with a glare that stabs like a pocketknife—not quite deadly, but painful enough.

I focus on the coloured blotches on my skin. So maybe my hands do look like a close-up of an impressionist landscape that Monet guy would paint, but Velvet doesn't need to get snooty about it. Or try to crack off my fingers, which would be death to a sign painter, even one in training, and not so great for a cucumber picker either. "You're not exactly spotless yourself," I grumble.

Maybe I'm even a little disappointed in her for getting a bad art review.

"What did you say?" Velvet's face deepens to blood red. Her eyes force me to look away. "You ungrateful, filthy little—" She grabs an open paint tin and rears back with it, like she'll slosh the whole mess over my head if I don't revise my comment.

"I didn't say anything. And I'm not ungrateful." I shimmy backwards until my back is pressed against the cold wall. "I'm really and truly thankful for your guidance and support." My voice quivers. A burr from the cement block behind me drives through my T-shirt and presses against my back. "Thankful from, uh, the bottom of my heart ... to have this opportunity to work..."

Velvet pulls back the paint tin further.

"...with you."

Her grip tightens.

"And whatever is in your trunk or house is absolutely none of my business," I add.

The paint can lowers.

"I don't even remember what all was in there." I nod to the closed box. "Just some towels and crap."

Velvet's shoulders melt down as she returns the paint tin to the table.

I exhale and peel myself away from the cement wall.

With a look as blank and cool as the girl at McDonald's asking what you'd care to order, Velvet bends down in front of the trunk. "Why don't I take this?" She lifts up the dishtowel puddled on the floor, and with the merciless calm of a lioness over a gazelle's body, she rips the towel in half.

I slip around the table to pick up my brush and shake off the chill Velvet sent down my spine. Who cares what she stores in a trunk anyway? I bet even Picasso got bad reviews. After she's settled down—maybe tomorrow or the next day—I'll finish the Schellenberger sign, and even better, start one of my own.

"I should head home, Velvet." I make my voice cheerful. Normal, like nothing happened. "I have to help with dinner." With my brush, I hammer a jaunty beat in the can of turps. Orange billows in the can.

"Whatever suits you." Velvet neatly folds her recent victim of textile violence into quarters.

"Tomorrow I could come back. You know, at the usual time?"

"If you like." She returns to Norm's sign. Her footprint-in-progress is smeared, like it started off as a regular chicken hop but wound up careening out of control.

I still the hammering brush. "Sorry to make you mess up."

"I'll fix it."

The average person would require twenty-four hours to settle down from a minor explosion. Velvet seems calmer already.

Frito Lays. I'll bring cases full of them tomorrow.

I bike onto the shoulder of highway. When I look back, Velvet is still wiping away the frayed edges of her letter.

A FEW NIGHTS LATER, I'm in pajamas and standing before the full-length mirror in my bedroom. I pull earrings from a tiny brown bag. I have my own smart accessories now. Magnetic earrings. Silver-edged and dotted with red centres like miniature, jam-filled tarts. Just as delicious looking, too. The girl at the store promised me I'd love the wonder of fridge magnet technology. Earring front and back will cling together through my lobe. Magnetic earrings don't pinch like screw-ons or clip-ons either. In public, I'll be as pierced as the next girl, and then slip the jewellery into my pocket at the front door, purity and wholeness about my ears.

I finger the earrings in the palm of my hand. I'll wear them tomorrow when Velvet presents our sign to the Schellenbergers. So what if the big shots in the city don't appreciate her work? Norm will be so amazed when he sees our painted wonder that he'll lay an egg.

Velvet and I painted all yesterday afternoon. She didn't blow up even once. At first I wasn't sure about going back. I wondered if her last apprentice was a nice cucumber worker who couldn't form her letters properly so Velvet shot the poor little thing and buried her under the maple tree in the front yard. The idea got me chewing my thumbnails down to the tender parts, but then I realized that nothing exciting like that ever happens around Putnam, so I got down to work.

Mom and Dad's voices float up to my loft. I've been trying to ignore the arguing, but it's getting harder. I hold still.

"It's a family celebration, Gerald." Mom has the quaver in the voice she gets when Dad's driving her batty. "Did you forget your granddaughter's eighth birthday? Or were you hoping you could skip it and keep working on the seminars?"

Anna's birthday: check. While I was in town buying earrings, I got her a present too.

"Things are strained enough as it is with Doreen and Leonard," Mom continues. "They come so seldom. Having Debbie here will be awkward. You'll talk about work all the time."

Debbie? Not again.

"I can't keep track of dates," Dad says. He sounds offhanded and relaxed. "I'm not sure you even told me."

"I did."

"Remind me next time. I invited Debbie to come here for lunch on Saturday. That's all there is to it."

Debbie has been back twice since the day she and Dad snooped in my bedroom. Mom's been stormy about the extra cooking. I'm not sure Debbie and Dad's notions of expanding the Becker Institute for Success is sitting well with her either.

"She's not family," Mom says.

"That doesn't matter. She believes in the seminars. In positive thinking. She's even interested in part time work with the Institute while she's in school."

"For God's sake, Gerald, you don't have enough work to hire an employee."

"I know a good attitude when I see it. Maybe buying property is a little over our heads, but thanks to Debbie, I have a new business concept."

"Oh, Gerald. I don't want to know."

"It's too exciting to bear. I know. This project will really take off."

Thank God I have a place to paint, away from this lunacy. I dig in the brown bag. I can't find an earring back.

"How much are we talking this time?" Mom's voice sounds worn, like a burlap bag, holey and saggy from carrying too much.

"Not much, especially when you consider what the project will bring in."

Mom's sigh travels up to the bedroom. "I'm going to bed."

I shake my head, hear a ting on the floor and crouch down to hunt for my missing left earring. I mustn't have positioned it right.

"I'll tell you what," Dad says. "Debbie and I will make homemade ice cream for the party. I wouldn't mind the chance to test her out with a hands-on project anyway. Find out if she's a real worker."

"Just get the lights, will you?"

I catch sight of a glimmer of earring bit, swipe it off the floor and hurl it into the garbage. Stupid magnet idea. Some crazy notion that sounds good until you try it, probably like Dad's new project. I drop onto the bed and pull up the sheets. Slowly turn to my other side, so the bedsprings don't groan. They complain anyway.

"Martha?" Dad calls up. Seconds later, he jogs up the steps. "Still awake?"

"I am now." I yawn sleepily, a cover for eavesdropping.

"I'm not sure if you heard your mother and me." His voice falls quiet as Mom's footsteps clomp to their bedroom.

I heave my quilt over my shoulders and stare blankly at the wall. Do not engage in discussion with him, I tell myself. Whatever you say, he'll overpower you with positive thinking.

"You know how anxious your mother gets. It's her personality. Change is hard on her. Young people embrace change so much more easily." Dad squats on the floor in front of me. He pauses long, a theatrical tool he used in sermon delivery. "I haven't had a chance to tell your mother details about my new project for The Becker Institute for Success."

I say nothing. That wall of mine could use some touch up work.

"But I can tell you this much: we'll need your help in designing the visuals." Dad is helpless to the excitement swelling in his voice. "Something mammoth. Uplifting. Something spectacular." Joy sparkles in his eyes. "I'm commissioning you, Martha. Just like I promised."

I fake another yawn. I'd rather pick a hundred acre farm of cucumbers than work for Dad. None of his projects work out, and they're always goofy.

"You're tired. We'll talk it over soon." He pats the covers.

I mumble a meaningless syllable and close my eyes. Thank God for Velvet. I think about the delivery of the sign tomorrow, and fall asleep to visions of the Schellenbergers' elated faces.

Chapter 10

THE NEXT DAY, I slip out the door early, before Dad can throw his Becker Institute net over my head. The cucumber field is broiling, but I'm too excited about the arrival of the Schellenberger sign to care.

Bernie tosses a cuke in the bushel basket positioned between us. "What did you get Anna for her birthday?"

I check the road in the distance for the seventeenth time. "I wanted to get her a Shera, Princess of Power Doll, but I decided against it."

"Naa. Doreen wouldn't go for Shera."

A red truck crests the hill.

"She's here!"

Bernie twists to look. "Who?"

"Velvet!" The sign is propped in the back of her truck and cloaked in a flapping blanket. Slowly, as though any sudden move could jar the treasured cargo, she veers onto Bernie's laneway.

"I forgot she was coming." Bernie rips off her garden gloves and tosses them on the cucumbers heaped in the basket. As she scurries across the field toward the truck, I skip along beside her, my heart dancing. Then I check myself and calm to a civilized gait. Must look casual. Only quietly curious.

"Velvet's been secretive," Bernie says as we work our way across the field. "She told my dad he'd love the design so much he wouldn't need to see a plan. We have no idea what she's been up to."

"Really?"

Suddenly, Bernie stops to clamp a lid on her excitement, too. "Too bad we didn't use the sketch you made on the Cheerios box." Her eyes are overflowing with apology. "Too bad we couldn't give you the break."

"Oh, Bernie." I laugh and coax us forward. "I forgot all about that sketch." I don't tell her our new design is my own brainchild. She'll be so surprised.

Bernie breathes out relief. "Are you sure?"

I give ol' Bern a light smack upside the deltoid muscle. "Let it go. Seriously. I have other things on my mind."

"Like what? Or who? *John?*" Then Bernie does something highly weird. She stops at the edge of the field and leans into me with a sultry shoulder rub. "Is John filling up your head? Or is he filling up other parts?"

"Bernie!" Shocked, I back up a step or two and even forget about Velvet's arrival. Bernie doesn't do sex talk. It fits her bad, like too-big shoes your heels keep slopping out from.

"What's wrong? Aren't you two having any fun?"

I stare at Bern, her generous nose and pink face. Something big and thrilling is pulsing behind her smile and trying to squeeze out. "We're having all the fun we want," I say. Slowly. Soberly. "Why? Is anything on *your* mind?" Leanne and Tammy Mills's tall tale of a secret lover echoes at the back of mine.

"Girls!" Bernie's dad yells from beside the truck. "Move your rears."

Bernie upgrades to a trot and takes the lead. I follow her past the barn and down the gravel embankment. Past the house, where her mother is setting down flats of eggs on the porch and turning toward the Great Sign Unveiling. Velvet is sliding the ratchet straps off the blanketed sign. I pick up the pace.

Bernie yells, waving madly. "Wait for us!"

We sprint down the gravel lane. She jostles in front of Norm for priority viewing before the sign. She blocks my view, but it's more important to have a clear sight of the Schellenberger faces. I shift so I can see them all.

"Drum roll?" Velvet requests as she unbuckles the last strap. "Who's got sticks?"

"This'll be interesting." Bernie's mother checks her watch.

Bernie and her parents wait before the covered sign. I utter a silent prayer for full chorus Schellenberger rejoicing.

"Pull it off," Bernie says.

"Sure you want to see this?" Velvet, grinning, holds the bottom of the blanket—the thin divide between our masterpiece and their hopeful faces.

Bernie smiles at me, her eyes shimmering. I hold in an enormous smile.

With the flourish of a Spanish toreador, Velvet gives a whoop and draws back the blanket. The letters sparkle in the sun. The chicken footprints dance in their wondrous wallpaper of poultry patterning.

Norm scratches his ear. Bernie's mom's eyes drop to gravel driveway. There's silence.

"Whoa," says Bernie, finally. "Chicken feet. Everywhere!"

"Well, well, well." Norm coughs awkwardly. "Isn't that something?"

I search his eyes but come up empty.

"I'll get the chequebook," her mom says. "Get that part out of the way."

Velvet hasn't pulled her gaze away from our sign. "It's an *avant garde* approach, but trust me, ladies and gentlemen, you won't tire of it."

As Bernie's mom toddles to the house, and Norm shoves his hands in his pockets and starts whistling at the sky, a horrible realization wells up in me.

"I nearly forgot the best part," Velvet says. "Martha Becker—"

"Is thrilled with the design," I butt in. "I hope to see more designs like this. Well, not exactly like it, but you know, with horse prints or cow hooves. They'll be the next big thing." I hesitate. "Maybe."

"Fun," Bernie says evenly. "Anyway, we should get back to work."

I can't look at Velvet. I follow Bernie along the path to our cucumber rows and trip over a clod of dirt on the way. I feel like a wasted partygoer the day after. "They hate the sign, don't they?" I say to Bernie's back.

"Not necessarily. You know my parents. Not the type to holler and jump up and down over art. I thought the design was cool."

"Really?" A small light ignites in my heart.

"Kind of. Weird-cool. Like that hairy little sheet Leanne showed us after she got her bikini line waxed the first time."

The light blinks off.

"What did you think of the sign?" Bernie stops at a wooden stake for marking the start of a cucumber row.

"It didn't make sense for your family." I look back across the field to Velvet and Bernie's parents, deep in conversation. Velvet pulls the blanket over the sign, like a sheet over a dead body. I could crawl under it too, and let the scratchy covering numb the bigger pain. So what if a zany artist likes my designs? The public hates them.

"We should have used your design on the Cheerios box," Bernie says.

I ignore Bernie's comment, grab a thorny vine and rip off another cucumber.

I FIND VELVET CURLED INTO A FETAL POSITION on the cement floor of her carport. She's probably been lying there since this morning's visit to the Schellenbergers. "Velvet?" I crouch down and check for signs of life.

"You were so good with the chicken." Her voice is small and muffled.

"Bernie says her dad doesn't jump up and down about art, that's all." I have to be strong for her. I'll bleed out my own grief later.

Velvet seems to swallow back a sob. "He hated the sign."

"You don't know that."

"He said it was too 'out there' and could I please paint him a simpler one. What in hell is simpler than dipping a chicken's feet in paint and letting it hop around your sign?"

"The bastard."

"Did he appreciate my sensitive observations of his nature? Embrace my—our—painterly rendition of his true self? No."

I stand up, brush dust off my shorts and assess the unfinished projects in the shop. "I could paint the background on the Neubrandt sign. You rest. Have some quiet."

Velvet pulls her knees in tighter and her circle shrinks more. "You know what Norm wants? Black lettering. Stunt-your-growth-from-lack-of-stimulation black letters on white ground." She rocks a little, like she's soothing herself. "Shoot me now. Before Norm Schellenberger and all the dead weight around here suck the life out of me."

As I move to the supply table, I look forward to leaving Velvet's place and never looking back. I'm not artist material. I don't have what it takes. But for now, Velvet needs support. "Maybe people around here are too uptight for *avante garde* ideas," I say. "Maybe they need tamer ones."

Velvet unfurls herself from her ball of misery. She rests her knuckles on the floor, like a gorilla. Rises to her knees and with determination, stands up. "No, Martha."

"No, what?"

"Our creative forces—swirling from within like a wellspring of life—will not be tamed."

When I find the paint roller and check its wooly surface, it hits me. All I'm good for are basics like harvesting vegetables. Or applying flat areas of paint, which is so head-crushingly boring I'll give it up after the next coat. "I'll put down the background on the Neubrandt sign. Then I'll head out, if you think you'll be okay."

Smiling fiercely, Velvet grabs a paintbrush off the table and jabs it into the air. "You and I weren't born to make labels for livestock, Martha. You and I—you, especially—were born to make statements. Statements that drive into the centre of one's being like a blade slicing open a carcass. Born to tell *truths.*" She lets the word dangle in the air for a moment, like a sign swinging from two chains.

I scan the paint tins, pull one out and tap the label. "The dairy farmers want a beige background, don't they?"

Velvet waves off the can and nabs a stool. Twirls it around on one leg and hops on. "Close your eyes, Martha. Tell me. What message is burrowing in the deepest chasm of your soul?"

"I'm not much of an idea person." I set the can down, cross my arms and sigh. "I'm no good at that stuff. Just ask Norm Schellenberger."

"It's not up to you to decide if you're good or worthy." Velvet clasps her hands like she's begging me to understand. "That's other people's jobs. You're an artist. It's your job to create." Then she lets her hands drop to her lap and sits tall. "Close your eyes."

I don't have the energy. "Why can't you be the deep artist?"

"Trust me. If I could, I would."

I remember her art review in the newspaper and wish I hadn't said anything.

Velvet's fingers gnarl up into fists. "I'm trapped, Martha," she carries on, "like a caged animal. I *have* to give people what they want. I have rent due next week. Bills coming out my south end. But you? You've got three meals a day set in front of you. And your whole future ahead."

"You're not exactly a senior citizen."

"I'm twenty-three years old, Martha."

"So why do you keep growing older around here when you could be back in the city? People love crazy shit there. My friend Leanne even told me."

Velvet snorts softly. Then she looks hollow suddenly, her eyes vacant. "I can't go back."

"Why not?" She could work toward better art reviews.

"It's too late." Just as suddenly, Velvet flinches back to life. "Paint your way out of this hellhole. Go to art college. Make something of yourself, Martha Becker."

I pick at a bit of paint crusted on the edge of the paint roller. "I'll probably stick around here with John. In a couple of years, he'll buy up property. Maybe there'll be space for a cucumber plot." My words sound empty, like a story read aloud to a kid who isn't listening. "Or I could grow pearl onions," I add weakly. "I hear Lowe's is looking for those too."

"For the last time, close your eyes."

Without the strength to resist, I shut them. At least the darkness quiets the mash of thoughts tumbling in my head. The view inside my mind grows blank and dark. Empty, like your average moment of shut-eye.

"Let the ideas come when they're ready," Velvet croons. "Still your mind. What message is knocking at the door? Plaintive at first, but then with persistent vigor, banging relentlessly to be set free?"

I sway back and forth on the chair. "I want my ears pierced." I told her I was no good with ideas.

"Oh. Okay," she says slowly, like she's trying to divine value from my airhead idea. "Let's try again. Do you envision a massive sign or a smaller one? Try and see it."

"Not too big a sign," I say, my eyes scrunched shut. "I wouldn't want to look demanding."

"Keep watch, Martha. You're beginning a journey into a place so vast the acres never end. Your mind's eye. Look for a truthful sign. Not a pretty, perfect one in Roman letters and respectable colours, but a meaningful, inner message that needs to be told."

A few sparkles flit across the screen in my mind. "Welcome to The Becker Institute of Success and Higher Consciousness?"

Velvet groans. "Don't tell me. Your dad's concoction?"

"Yeah."

"Keep looking."

"It's dark in here," I complain. I cover my eyes to stop them from opening.

"Anything now?"

"Just static. Wait!" Out from the darkness, bold words come burning though, like the nighttime glow from a living room window with the TV on.

"What is it?"

"I can see a message, Velvet. It's forming." Miraculously.

"Excellent."

"It's a road sign. Square, low to the ground. Small, like an eight-by-eight pan for Rice Krispie squares."

"Good."

I press my palms against my eyelids. "And the sign is feathered in grassy brush strokes. You can barely notice the difference between the strokes and the weeds in the ditch." Prickles jitter along my nerves.

"Keep going."

"There's an arrow pointing straight at our house. Past the bricks and mortar to the desk where my dad works."

"And?"

The pulse discos down to my heart and throbs like the club in Thorndale we snuck into last spring. "And the sign, ever so faintly, says...."

"Says what, Martha?"

I lean over and whisper in her ear.

I open one eye, which Velvet doesn't notice because she's gripping her head in a kind of stunned ecstasy, and then I open the other. She slumps back in her stool like she's been walloped.

"That's good, Martha. I like that one. I like it a lot."

"You do?"

"It's a truth. Not a corny ad everyone's heard too many times. I want to see your message move out from your imagination and into the world."

Suddenly, I feel loud and gaudy, like oversized, cheap earrings. "What if someone saw it?"

Atop her stool, Velvet folds up her legs like a Buddhist goddess, if there is such a thing. She places her hands in prayer and gazes ceiling-ward. "True art creates an audience."

"Audiences don't want insane stuff like that."

"Do you think paintings by the Group of Seven are insane?"

I roll my eyes. "They're landscapes."

"At first they were considered outrageous. Artists are leaders. Boundary pushers." Velvet unfolds her legs, slips off the stool and breezes over to the jumbled stack of off-cuts looming against the wall in the shadows. "I've got lots of extra panels. Find the one you need. Take a couple, in case inspiration strikes."

I slide forward in my stool and dip my toe on the floor.

"Go."

I edge closer to the panels propped against the wall and flip the first board toward me. Flip another. And another, until a shiver snakes down my spine, because the next board is square, probably eight by eight inches, and exactly like the one I imagined. I reach down to pull it out, and picture the painted words coming to painfully beautiful life.

Chapter 11

WAVES LAP ONTO THE SHORE in front of us. The blood red sun—a giant sky-cyclops hovering over the horizon—beams us straight on. Except for a few walkers in the distance, strolling the beach and dragging sticks, John and I are alone. We forgot a blanket again, but a cluster of smooth rocks at our spines works as chairbacks.

John and I watch the clouds shift and blend into each other. He slides his hand under the sleeve of my sweater and I nestle against his shoulder; inhale the warm, soapy, just-stepped-out-of-the-shower-smell he manages to hold onto for hours.

"Maybe you figured it out," he almost whispers. "What I have to tell you."

Soft breezes rustle the grasses behind us. I rub my palm over his chest. "Don't tell me. A new lawn sprinkler?"

"We could use one of those revolving ones. No. Something more significant."

My hand stills, and the truth hits me. And it's perfect. John is ready. Finally, we've found our perfect, red sky evening. Once we're together, all my doubts about our relationship—which were meaningless, really—will disappear. John and I will truly be one. I wonder if he brought protection.

I move my hand low. Arc it over his navel and breathe a deep inhalation of John-ness. "Really?"

His gaze floats to the clouds. "Really."

A path behind us leads to a clearing with grasses growing up from the sand. We could wander back. Or strip down and drift into the water. It's almost dark enough. Can you have sex in a lake? Or would John shrivel up from the water, like soaked toes in a bathtub? I stroke his shirt and wonder. "Can I ask you something first?"

"Sure." His gaze pulls away from the sky.

"You haven't had sex with anyone else, right?" I'm ninety-eight percent sure he hasn't. That's what's good about Trekkie farmer guys. They don't usually have a long list of lovers a girl has to compare herself to.

"No. Not really."

Just as I thought. I yank my hand back. "What do you mean, not *really*?"

John kisses the rim of my ear. "No one special."

I pull off my sandal and shake out the grit. "Anyone not special?"

John tosses a nervous glance to a length of driftwood a few feet away. "There was one, but she was exceptionally not special."

I shimmy back a little so I can view his face better. John? With another lover? I should be jealous, but I'm too surprised. And above all else, curious. "Who was it?"

He waves my question aside.

"Who?"

"Just ... Cheryl," he mumbles, and brushes off a gathering of sand from a crease in his jeans.

"Cheryl Meyer?" With the scrub brush hair? Always rushing down the halls at school like she was late for a doctor's appointment? "I knew you two were friends." Shouldn't my predecessor in love be more popular and attractive? "Was it amazing? Or just regular? Or awful? And where? Where did you do it?" I need details to bring this strange, nearly impossible fact to life.

"Do we have to talk about this?" John crosses his arms and leans back against the rock. "Tonight?"

"Yes."

He looks to the sun as though it'll lend him strength, and begins. "It only happened once. Okay, twice. Cheryl Meyer is a good and kind person, and we've known each other since—I don't know. Sunday School. But it was more like a science experiment for both of us. I was comfortable with her. That's all."

Cheryl Meyer: Kind. Good. Comfortable. Slowly, a dark and fierce acid I never knew I had rises up from some bitter, bile producing organ deep inside me, probably near my large intestine. I never did like Cheryl Meyer. Did I? I'm sure I didn't. An image glares in my mind. "Did you do it in your bedroom?" Was Cheryl Meyer's pale flesh between John's plaid sheets?

"No." Impatiently, he swishes his running shoe across the ground.

Phew. "Then where?" I aim for pleasant. Cheerful even, so he'll co-operate, but silently, I resolve never to have sex anywhere remotely associated with Cheryl Meyer.

"You really want to know?"

"Really."

John sighs. "The first time was in the library."

I gasp. "School or town?" The dark acid trickles away and my curious brain takes control.

"Town. Not by the bookshelves or anything. Just in the bathroom."

"Seriously? The one near Adult Fiction?"

"No, the other one. By the reference books at the back," he says, like he's giving directions to a street address.

"I never knew there was a bathroom back there." Awe overtakes me. John and Cheryl. In the library.

"The door isn't that visible. That's what made it easier."

"Did you two slip into a stall and lock the door behind you?"

"We don't need to get into details, Martha. I've already said too much."

"I guess a bathroom would be handy in case you need to wash up after." I sit back and look to the horizon, a steady place to calm my jumble of feelings.

"Can we talk about something else?" John sounds suddenly tired.

"What about the other time?"

"It doesn't matter."

"You can't stop now, John. Once you start something you have to finish." I try sounding motherly to guilt him into telling me, because damn it, I have to know the rest.

He scratches the back of his head and wiggles the toe of his running shoe in the sand.

"Please?"

"It was in her family's backyard one night. In their swimming pool."

"So you *can* have sex in the water." To hell with the gentle waves in front of us. We're not going in there, thank you very much.

"You were wondering?"

"Never mind. Wow, John." I turn and look at him afresh. John MacIntosh, with the scandalous, sexy past. He looks older. More mature. "So did you two sign out books after, or did you go straight home?"

"Stop. I don't know how we got onto this." He exhales a gust of frustration. "Martha. I've been wanting to talk to you about something."

My insides go squishy. Sickish feeling. "I don't think we can have sex tonight, John. I just can't get the picture of Cheryl—"

"I wasn't saying we should." John swings his whole self around to look at me. "That's not what I've been trying to tell you."

I freeze, then ping-pong my eyes north and south across the horizon. "It isn't?" I can't look at John. Carefully, I ease the sleeve of my sweater down and smooth it over my wrist. I can't even look near him.

He pauses and says, "I figured you knew, Martha. I've mentioned the place enough times. I went ahead. I bought the farm." In my side vision, he's reining back a smile, like he needs to see my reaction before he can let it go.

The importance of John's sex adventures drain away like grains of sand through fingers. "A farm?" I eye him suspiciously. "Already? How'd you do that?"

"I signed my name a dozen times and wrote a cheque with lots of zeroes." John lets his smile loose. "I didn't want to say anything until I was sure."

"Where did you get the zeroes?" What kind of an eighteen-year-old buys a farm anyway?

"Investments did well this year. My parents helped too." John's chest inflates. He seems to be enjoying the view of my questions bouncing around the beach.

"No kidding." I slump back against the rock. The sun's electric reds and oranges have dwindled to a dull, khaki-coloured haze. A chill is settling in the air.

"Fifty acres. Mostly workable," he adds. "North of here, in Ridley Township."

"I thought you were just exploring the countryside. Finding landscapes for your story settings. Places where aliens land or something. I didn't think you'd buy something so soon." I pull up my legs and hug them. "What about university?"

"I'm not going to bother."

"What?"

"I didn't think the sale would happen this fast either," John continues, "but the place came on the market. It was too good a deal." His voice goes silky. "I mentioned the house, didn't I?"

I don't want to look at him or think about the responsibility of a house and a grown-up relationship.

"Three bedrooms," he adds. "The kitchen needs work. Land is hilly in those parts, but there's an area perfect for a small crop. Like cucumbers."

Or maybe I should set wacky sign painting aside. Consider the alternatives. "Close to the house, or do you have to walk half-way around the earth to get to it, like at Bernie's?"

"Close."

"Really." I turn the idea of John's farm over in my mind, like a shovel checking under the ground for potential in the soil.

"You're surprised I got a farm so soon," John says. "It's a risk. Believe me, I know. But when I saw the place ... "

I look at John. He almost turns shy.

"I could picture us there," he says.

The murmur of lapping waves fills our silence. Waves like John, ferrying me away to a farm in Ridley township. "What did you say the house was made of? Wood?"

"Brick. Yellow brick. Your mom would have a name for it. Ontario Gothic or something."

I love yellow brick houses. Living in one with John would be so much easier than leaving Putnam to become an artist of high regard. I should be thrilled. Except I can't inhale full lungs worth of air. Shallow. Breathing. Is all I can. Manage.

John's arm pulls me back in. "I know," he says softly. "It's a lot to think about."

I groan.

"It's Cheryl, isn't it?" he asks. "See? I knew I shouldn't have said anything. Damn."

"No, John. Having sex in the library is impressive. Really." I give his leg a pat and turn my gaze to the sky. To the dying clouds, softening and fading until the last one sighs into the horizon and disappears.

Chapter 12

EIGHT WISPS OF SMOKE rise from the blown out candles on Anna's cake. John hung around our kitchen this morning while I trailed *Anna's Going Bananas!* on top in yellow icing, a nod to her favourite flavour. Writing with icing is highly satisfying. A safe, respectable outlet for graphic design, unlike painting off-colour remarks on signs. Thank God I'm over that. I've kept clear of Velvet's shop all week, and I'm not going back. Doreen is right. I'm exceptionally lucky to have John.

Although Doreen and the gang feel threatened by our family's non-Mennonite ways, they're putting religion aside today for the sake of Anna's birthday. Everyone is cozy around the dinner/communion table. Even though Debbie crashed the party and Mom is still silently fuming about her and Dad's business concepts, at least we're all together. And best of all, John is sitting next to me, his black-socked toes tucked under the arch of my bare foot and gently exploring its nether regions. This morning he even asked to see Doreen's rings. He plucked the engagement ring out of the pile and slipped it into his back pocket. Having a clear future ahead of you feels solid and secure.

Dad rises from the table and holds up his glass of red. He and Debbie are the only ones still wearing cone-shaped birthday hats. "One more toast before cake. No. Two. First, to John's new property. This young man, a mere—what are you, John? Eighteen?"

John nods.

Anna and Mary stare longingly at the banana cake in the center of the table, still uncut.

"At eighteen, this young man has purchased land. A success story. An example of positive thinking in action!"

"Didn't mean to cause a stir," John says, although he's stirring me up. I don't know what the business under the table is doing to him, but it's flooding me with pleasure not limited to my lower appendage.

"We're proud of you, John," Dad says. "Stand up, Ridley Township's Newest Land Owner. Speech!"

"No speech," John says. "Although I have to say ... a farm isn't home without someone to share it with." He smiles at me. When Doreen and Leonard look at each other, her eyebrows go up.

My heart balloons.

"That sounds wonderful," Dad says, but John's hint doesn't seem to register with him. Dad seems to have something else on his mind. "And for our second toast, to the Becker Institute of Success." Dad's eyes dart to Debbie, whose teeth have come out from hiding in a wide grin. "The institute is launching a new and exciting production." He pauses long enough to collect everyone's attention. "A video series! Recorded seminars for success, packaged in a boxed set, will soon be available for purchase across the nation!"

"Oh, Gerald," Mom mutters.

Debbie's eyes dance around the table. "I'm helping with the camera work."

Doreen and Leonard exchange more looks.

I wonder how much this gig will cost. But I have happier thoughts to occupy me. As Dad drones on, I slide the cake plate my way and cut it into wedges before Anna salivates all over the table and drowns us all. The cake feels like a celebration for me, too. Finally the confusion rattling my brain is gone. I *will* marry John. Sexy, foot-massaging John. I'll help run the farm and live in his blessed, yellow brick house, where we'll rub all kinds of body parts over top of each other.

"The series will encapsulate all my work to date," Dad babbles on.

John leans in tight, points to a slice of cake and whispers, "I scratched a heart on that piece when you weren't looking. It's for you."

I hand out plates of cake, sure to give myself the one with the heart, the sweetest drawing John ever gave me.

"Is there ice cream?" Mary asks.

"Reverend Gerald and I tried to make some," says Debbie, "but it didn't turn out as good as we hoped."

"It looked like soupy yogurt," Mom says, her voice frosty.

"I've even developed a visual concept for the institute," Dad continues, his volume mounting. "And this is where Martha comes in. Can everyone look up at the ceiling?"

The ceiling?

Anna and Mary obey. Skeptically, I look at John.

Dad points to the wooden slats above us. Way up. "See that space?"

The rest of us lift our gazes.

"That's where Martha will paint the sign for the Becker Institute."

"Sure, sure," I say. This too shall pass.

"Really?" says Debbie. "You never told me about this part, Reverend Gerald."

"I'm sure everyone is familiar with Michelangelo's famous painting in the Sistine Chapel," Dad says. "*The Creation of Adam.*

The glorious image of the white bearded God, floating in the sky and extending his finger to touch Adam's hand."

Dad will *not* ask me to paint the *Creation of Adam* on our ceiling. Even for him, it's too left field.

"Martha will paint an exact replica on the ceiling of our own Putnam Chapel!" Dad says.

What? Forget it. No siree.

"And underneath the vision of hope, she'll paint: *The Becker Institute for Success.* I've just commissioned her!" With arms outstretched for his final announcement, Dad awaits a shower of applause.

No one speaks.

"Dad," I protest. "I'm not Michelangelo."

"You can be if you want to." He gives me the ol' fist-cheer and sits down.

I hear Leonard mumbling something about "ridiculous."

"How's she going to get up there, Grandpa?" Anna asks.

"Ladders? Scaffolding? Ropes? Whatever it takes. And to start and close each video, the camera will pan," Dad points his imaginary camera up, "to a shot of the magnificent ceiling."

John's eyes lift. "That ceiling is a long way up."

"I'm not going up there." The muscles in my shoulders clench.

"It's not so high," Debbie says, her head tilted up.

"Martha can *not* go up there, Gerald," Mom says.

"We'll find a way." Dad shoots me a smile, and when we lock eyes, I know. Sometime soon, I'll be dangling from the ceiling, mountain climbing gear cinching my waist and a brush in hand. Once again, I'll do exactly what I'm told.

Zombie-like, I lift my fork from the table, spear a hunk of cake and down it. Stab another gob and stuff it in. I used to love banana cake. This time, I taste nothing.

John jerks his head down. "Martha? You ate the cake." He yanks his foot away.

"So we can start?" Anna sinks a fork in her piece and levers off a chunk.

An almost volcanic tremor overtakes John. What the hell? His face is turning a strangely neon red, but he hasn't started dessert. He can't be choking.

"John?" Leonard says. "Are you okay?"

"Stop eating, Martha!" John yells and grabs my hand.

"Thith cake ith good," Mary says, her mouth full.

"The engagement ring." Panic shivers in John's voice. "I slipped it in Martha's slice of cake!"

Doreen gasps.

I go rigid for a second. I lean over, open up and let the warm, gooey wad in my mouth poop back onto the plate with a soft whump. I poke it with my fork. Nothing.

"Gross," says Debbie quietly.

"You ate the ring?" Leonard sounds pissed.

"It must be in here somewhere," I say. While everyone's heads bend toward the remaining cake on my plate, John and I devastate the wedge with smashing, frantic forks.

We all stare at the mound of ransacked crumbs.

I imagine the x-ray of my esophagus and the ominous, ringed shadow. I hold my stomach.

"I wanted you to find it," John says, numb. "Here, with everyone together. I didn't think you'd eat like such a *machine*."

That was just rude. The hairs on the back of my neck go stiff.

"Can't this family do anything normal?" Doreen says.

"You could find the ring later," Anna offers helpfully.

"Double gross," Debbie says.

Everyone shushes, thanks to the collective image of me searching for Doreen's ring in the toilet. Even Mary stops eating.

"Can everyone stop looking at me?" I say. "It's Anna's birthday. Can't we give her presents?"

"Oh, yes!" says Dad. "Let's not dwell on Martha's little digestive problem. Do we have something for Anna, Peggy?"

"I'd have brought something," Debbie says to Doreen, "but I didn't know we were celebrating a birthday."

My mother balances her cup over her lap. Nervous waves ripple through the surface of her coffee. She didn't show even a glimmer of happiness over my future with John. Maybe she's too worried about the price tag on Dad's video series to let our news register. John's foot returns under the arch of mine, but I'm too stunned to care now. Down with the slimy bile and diamond solitaire engagement ring, a queasy truth swirls inside me: My marriage to John is off to a miserable start.

I reach under the table and hand Anna a wrapped gift. "Here," I grunt.

"The girls have all they need," Leonard says, but Anna's already clawing at the polka-dotted paper.

"We're pulling back on gifts altogether," Doreen adds curtly.

"Hush, Doreen," Dad says. "What have you got there, Anna?"

Anna unsheathes the newest edition of *Far Side* comics.

"It's got lots of cows and chickens," I manage to say though the still thick fog in my brain. "You see the world from the animals' points of view."

Anna beams me a smile through the fog and cracks open the front cover.

"I can't see." Mary tucks in closer.

"Very kind, Martha." Doreen lifts the book from Anna's hand and closes the cover. She drops the book in the shadows under her pew.

"Doreen!" Dad says. "Let's all share passages from the *Farther Edge.*"

"The *Far Side*," I murmur.

"Cartoons aren't in line with our thinking anymore." Leonard's voice drops. Trembles a little. "And neither is carelessness with valuable jewelry."

"I had no idea she'd—" John begins.

"Or silly ideas of painting on ceilings," Doreen adds.

Dad bristles.

"Would anyone mind if I helped myself to seconds?" Debbie asks Mom.

"Go ahead," she replies, torturing a hangnail.

"We just want a simple life," Leonard says. "None of these grandiose business schemes and pointless gifts."

"Leonard." Dad's eyes are bright as he leans toward him. "Try to disregard negative thoughts. Instead, visualize images of strength and power. You can do it!"

Leonard's eyes cool. "Girls?" His lips barely move. "It's time to go."

"Oh, boy," John mutters, and all of a sudden, Doreen is up and pressing the girls toward the door, her skirts swishing violently. Leonard crowds behind them, herding them forward.

I shove my mashed cake away and hurry after them. I'm out of the fog, but now the room is too clear. Too vividly messy. "You can't go. It's Anna's birthday!"

"Sorry, Martha," Doreen says, as the girls jostle out the door and pile into their black car. "The cake was excellent. Next time, come to our place. It's calmer there." She lets the screen door bang shut behind her and without looking back, climbs into the car.

John comes up behind me. "Anna's right," he says softly. "You can find the ring in a day or two."

The last thing I want to do is dig through the stinking remains of the worst birthday party ever.

"That roast was incredible, Mrs. Becker," Debbie says from somewhere behind me. "No worries about the ice cream. We'll figure out how to crank that thing next time!"

One last wedge of cake is left standing on the table. *Anna's Going Bananas.* It was all wrong. Not Anna at all.

I close my eyes. Images of signs begin to fester and boil. Wicked signs for John's new farm and Doreen's house. Signs for all of Putnam's lunacy start tumbling in my head, and this time, I know. There's only one way to get rid of them.

Chapter 13

VELVET RUMBLES ALONG THE HIGHWAY, her arm draped out the driver's side window. I lean over and check the speedometer. It feels like we're crawling, although she's going the speed limit. "I just hope the sign doesn't get ripped off by the time we get there."

"Are we talking about signage not adhering to municipal bylaws by any chance?"

I bounce my leg nervously. "Yeah."

"I wondered." She cranks up the tunes on the radio. "Who'd have thought you'd be leading an art tour?" she says over the music. "Just this morning, I was thinking I'd never see you again, Martha Becker. What's it been, a week and a half since you graced my doorstep?"

"About that."

"I was sure you'd lost all interest in the production of fine art."

"Or not so fine. A bit rough around the edges, actually." I rub the back of my neck. Since Dad keeps insisting I paint *The Creation of Adam* on our ceiling, I've realized I have to take control of my artistic direction. "I needed time to think."

Velvet gears down for a hulking yellow combine clogging the road ahead of us.

"Move it, dinosaur," I yell across the windshield. "Stay in the field where you belong." More sweetly, I inquire, "Could you pass him, Velvet?"

When she does, I remember to slouch down in my seat and slide on my sunglasses, not that they'll disguise me, but I'll take a false sense of security over nothing.

Velvet, smiling, pops open the glove compartment and pulls out a pair for herself. "Going undercover? Let me play. No one will ever know it's me." She shakes her spikes of hair and laughs.

"Don't make yourself obvious, that's all."

"Like this?" she says, fishtailing left and right across the road until I have to grab onto the door handle to keep myself from knocking against the side of her truck.

"Velvet! Jesus."

"I'm just happy to see you. God, Martha. It feels like years. Look! *Rancrest Farms*," She reads off the sign on our right. "The lettering is exhausted and the Holstein is faded. Shall we offer the Rancrests a business card?"

"Later. We're getting closer." Adrenaline surges and pulses the hairs at the back of my neck.

"There's another one: *Sweet Corn for Sale*. Looks like little Johnny's first time with a paintbrush. Not your calling, kid!" she calls out the window to no one in particular.

"Quit it, Velvet." A car swishes past us and I slip deeper in the seat. "Keep going straight, just past my place. There. Slow down." I check around for surveillance systems recently installed on hydro poles, hovering helicopters or nosey locals lurking behind trees. I can see the sign, but I don't stare, so as not to give away its exact location.

Velvet eases onto the gravel shoulder, turns down the radio and shuts off the engine. Sounds of twittering birds fill the void.

"See anything unusual?" I ask.

She scans the vista past the windshield. Her eyes rove from the speed limit sign ahead to the back of the sign for Putnam in the distance. "No."

"Good. I wasn't too obvious." Painting the sign was like stomping down the stinking bullshit in my life, especially the kind I get from my dad, and growing something out of it. Something green and alive—and not for Lowe's Pickles, either, but for me.

"So I *am* hunting for your sign."

"Absolutely."

Velvet's eyes focus. She lets go a breath of astonishment. "Good Lord, Martha."

"What do you think? Honestly?" Poking out from the tall weeds in the ditch, my sign stands a few feet off the ground, a sturdy square no bigger than a cake pan and hammered onto a garden stake. It's green and striped in reedy veins, barely noticeable against the waving grasses, but if you squint hard, you can see the letters buried like hidden shapes you hunt for in a kid's activity book.

While Velvet sits, speechless, a new fear sets in. She might like my sign about as much as the Schellenbergers liked theirs.

"*False Hopes, Turn Right,*" Velvet reads. She stares in silence for a good minute. "A simple yet scathing commentary on society's need to cram excellence down people's throats. I love it."

My insides glow.

"How'd you post that thing anyway?"

"There was enough moonlight to see last night."

Velvet yelps. "You worked under the moon?"

"I snuck out of the house after my dad started snoring. Carried the sign under one arm and the sledgehammer in the other." I toss off the sunglasses so I can admire the sign with clarity.

"What if someone pulled over?"

"No one saw me. As far as I know, no one's seen the sign, either."

Velvet creaks open the truck door. "I'll rescue it."

"From what?" I check for cars, climb out of the truck and follow her. "Leave it, Velvet."

She stands in the weedy grass and slides her hands under the edges of the sign. "People could spot this baby and have their way with it. Toss it in the back of a van or some other place equally nasty." She heaves on the board.

I reach protectively for the sign. "You can't pull it out. I banged it in hard."

But with one last wrench, Velvet breaks the stake free from the ground. I watch her carry the sign to the back of her truck, lay it flat and nestle it with the woolen blanket she draped over Norm's chicken farm sign two weeks ago. "This sign doesn't belong in somebody's woodpile, and that might just be where it ends up."

"How do you know? I liked looking at my sign posted up."

"Signs are vulnerable."

I hoist myself over the side of the truck and look down at my artwork, swaddled like a baby, small and innocent. Maybe Velvet is right. Maybe I should protect the little thing. I tuck the blanket in tighter where she missed a spot, and return to the cab.

Velvet moves to turn the key, but stops. She gazes out the window. "Martha." She sighs like she's got a big one to lay on me. "The voice of one subliminal sign doesn't have impact. Enough power. Influence. What you need is a sizeable collection."

"A collection?"

"A full choir." She jabs a thumb behind us. "This sign is just a beginning."

"You think so?"

"Painting the honest truth felt good, didn't it?"

"Awesome."

"Imagine the satisfaction of telling all, expressing in paint the dark, negative, miserable thoughts rumbling inside you and demanding to be let free."

"A collection of negative messages?" The potential beams hope inside me.

"Negative. Sarcastic. Mocking. Whatever you like."

"Yeah." I lay my head against the back of the seat and float the idea through my mind. "I could fill all the walls of your carport with signs."

"Think again, girl. Think bigger. Think all of Putnam." Velvet jerks around to face me. "You could blast the roadside with your *oeuvre*." Her eyes go glazy. "We could turn this old gravel shoulder into a contemporary gallery. *New Work*, by Martha Becker."

"Whoa. You can do that?" I give my head a shake. "You can't do that, Velvet."

"Who's stopping you?" Her eyes clear. "But I suppose if you'd rather," she says, drooping a hand over the steering wheel and picking at splatters on her skin, "you could paint up some sleepy landscapes instead. Enter one in the Putnam Fall Fair." She covers a yawn with the back of her hand. "Just don't blubber on my shoulder when the art schools you've been pining for look at your little autumn scene and fall into a coma."

"You don't think a show of road signs would be too obvious?"

Velvet erupts in laughter. "Isn't that what you want?"

"I guess." I sink lower in the seat.

She leans into the ignition, brings the engine to life and veers onto the highway. "If that's all the enthusiasm you can muster, don't even bother."

"A solo show is a huge step."

Velvet guns the motor. "I have to head back. Someone wants me to paint a sign for dairy goats."

"Wait." One of Dad's positive affirmations chatters in my ear. "I'll do it. I can. I *will* paint a bunch of signs."

"You sure?" Velvet checks her rear view. "A little art crime doesn't scare you off?"

"Crime?" Small print rules, probably. "Violating signage bylaws, you mean?"

Velvet hits highway speed and drapes her arm out the window. "A little slander. Libel. Depends how you go about it. But you'd be breaking the law in the name of art, which is part of the territory. I can't tell you how many leading-edge artists have stepped over legal boundaries—had to, really—to send a forceful message."

"Sure." Panic hammers my chest. Or excitement, maybe.

"You don't sound sure."

"Me? Nah. I'm sure." I stare ahead at the yellow line on the highway pulling us forward. Block out the rest of my thoughts about people's reactions, or making a dork of myself. Because I'm having a show. An art show. And those schools will see what serious commitment looks like.

Chapter 14

JOHN IS TOO BUSY INHALING the sight of his new property to notice my silence. As he pulls over along the side of the laneway, the tall grasses drag under the car. His yellow brick house stands alone, dwarfed by the fields and sky, like it'll never need the rest of the world for company. *Lonely Acres,* I'll label the place. My next sign. And the subtitle: *We specialize in ...* I look across the overgrown grass to the barn ... *Boredom and Emptiness.* Since Velvet helped me hatch the idea of a signage show along Putnam Road, graphic ideas have been appearing everywhere.

Today I'll tell John we're breaking up. I could feel sad if I let myself, but now is the time for strength and determination. As luscious as his skin is, as soft and dark his curls, I have to end our relationship. It's not right to lead him on or make him believe we'll wind up painting our names on his mailbox. I have an art career to launch, and I can't have a boyfriend who doesn't know Michelangelo from Picasso dragging me down.

A pointed gable pokes up from the roofline, trimmed in lacey wooden edging. It's a pretty house. Pretty like a diamond ring that belongs to someone else. A thing you idly, casually comment on and then look away and forget about, because the ring or the house or the life that goes with it has nothing to do with you or anything you care about.

"Cute," I say to fill-in-the-blank for my first impression. It's the best I can do. I'll walk through the place. Find details to compliment, maybe offer a congratulatory hug. Then I'll tell him.

John suddenly pivots in his seat like he's just remembered I'm here. "You didn't find Doreen's ring, did you? In any of your travels," he smiles weakly, "to the bathroom?"

"No." I don't look at him. "We'll have to let that one go."

"I guess that ring wasn't meant for us," he says with an easy shrug. "But I was thinking—"

"Is this the kind of landscape you wanted to write about for your new story?" Best to move the discussion away from the topic of "us."

John surveys his kingdom and seems to breathe in some pleasant odour I can't detect. "No time for hobbies now, but yeah. This place makes me think of a whole new planet."

"We're ten minutes from home, John."

"Far enough." He springs open the car door and jingles the keys. "Come on. I'll show you through."

John unlocks the front door and jives through the kitchen, humming and happily tapping on electrical outlets. "Needs new wiring. Dad can help."

An ochre yellow stripe pattern snakes up walls that look damp, and smell like an old dog, or maybe nursing home medication. I cough. "Interesting wallpaper," I say. "Very antique."

"Really?" John fingers the lip of a seam come undone. "I thought I'd start fresh."

The empty rooms echo our footsteps. An electric clock hangs on the wall. It's slightly askew and with faded gold spokes radiating from its face. A few short minutes until I tell John. "Nice they left you a clock."

"They're leaving all kinds of equipment in the barn and the shed, too. Generous and beyond." He turns for the basement stairs and pulls on the wobbly door knob. "You prowl around. I'll check the furnace." He bounces down the steps.

I climb the stairs to the second floor and peek into the master bedroom. Not that I'd wish a church-house on anyone, but I'm used to open spaces with cathedral type ceilings. The bedroom window here allows in a stingy rectangle of light.

I lean against the wall and lower myself to the carpeted floor. I've never seen John cry. I doubt he will today. He'll be strong, like always.

"Excellent choice of rooms to explore," he says from the doorway a few minutes later. He moves in close. At least his soap smell overpowers the stink of old dog, still upstairs. "You're quiet."

Fear skitters down my back. John could drag out my thoughts before I'm ready. "I'm always quiet," I say, quickly and a little too loudly. "You know me, girl of few words."

"That's not what I meant." He knocks on the side of my head like it's a front door. "Anybody home?"

I pull away.

"What's wrong? I know the place needs work."

"No! It's great, John. Just as it is." Maybe he will cry. Maybe I'll cry. Endings are hard even when they're for the best.

"The carpeting has to go." John waves a hand in front of his nose. "Just picture the place lived in, with a laundry basket in the corner and a vacuum cleaner in the closet."

"You fantasize about cleaning equipment?" Funny, silly John. I will miss him.

"Stop, Martha. You're getting me excited." He nuzzles my hair.

I can't find a smile for him. He licks my unpierced earlobe, which sparks a current of interest, but I ignore it.

The moment calls for honesty. I try and inhale courage. "I need to…" I need to tell him straight out. I look deep into his clear eyes. "You know that cool-looking shed?" I blurt out. "Could I see inside?" Damn. I'm more of a chicken than Norm Schellenberger's chickens.

"The shed?" John looks at me strange, stands up and starts downstairs. I follow him and close the front door behind us. As we cross the overgrown lawn, I promise myself to talk to him inside the shed. A shed is a place of work. Of getting things done.

But when John swings open the wooden shed door, we're flushed by the cool, morning garden smell inside. Birds lining the rafters flutter and fly circles at our arrival and settle back on their roosts. I move to the centre of the open space, stand still, and let my eyes adjust to the sunlight slipping through lengths of barn board and throwing stripes across the floor.

From a single round window, light streams in. "This place is amazing," I say.

"It wasn't a feature of the property I expected you to go soft on." John comes up from behind and puts his arms around me. "I don't know why I like you so much." His low tones massage into my back and settle in my chest.

"I have to talk to you." Tell him, for chrissake. It's just a hug in a shed. Soon I'll be skipping Putnam, whistling free and heading for the Big Smoke, a stack of paintings under my arm.

His arms slide across my stomach, up and up. His fingers skim my nipples. "Mm hmm?"

Tell him now, before …

His lips wet the nape of my neck and all my nerve endings, even the little ones that hide in the back, come into the sunshine to soak in the pleasure of John's touch. "John?" I say, more softly.

His hands slide over my hips and turn me around so his tongue can press into my mouth and the two of us—now one moving, pressing, wanting body—sink to the straw speckled floor. "You like the shed, huh?" he whispers, after he pulls his lips from mine.

"Feels good in here," I mumble, drunk-happy from his skin.

He draws back his head and his curls fall into silhouette against the sunlight slipping through slits in the roof. "Wouldn't you love to paint in here?"

Suddenly, a pressure from his knee I hadn't noticed drives into my thigh. He knows about my sign show. Or maybe it's just paranoia having its way with me. Either way, I push him back.

Undisturbed, John rubs my thigh with the palm of his hand. As his pressure deepens and moves higher, a glow of warmth and want radiates. "The place is perfect for painting," he adds in a breathy whisper. "There's even scaffolding."

I hold a stop sign hand against his chest. "Scaffolding?"

John motions his head toward the side wall.

I push him aside to see better.

A network of metal poles and stairs, clogged in spider webs, stands next to the wall. It looks like the skeleton of a prehistoric beast looming in the shadows.

"For climbing to high places," John adds. "Like ceilings. I bought it from the owners. Got a good price."

I groan and cover my eyes.

"What's wrong?" John leans back and rests his head on his hand. "Your dad isn't convinced about us, but I'll bring the scaffolding over. You'll paint the ceiling and he'll think I appreciate his interests."

"No." If John brings that stairway-to-hell to my house, I'll drown him in paint.

"You'll do fine, Martha. You can paint like—what's his name?"

"Michelangelo."

"I'm not sure how to take down scaffolding, but it can't be rocket science."

"Don't bother. I'm not painting the *Creation of Adam*." I pick bits of straw off my T-shirt. My words seem lost on John, already standing and hiking to the scaffolding to examine its hardware.

I fold an arm behind my head and gaze at the pigeon lined rafters. I can't imagine breaking apart scaffolding and rebuilding it at our house, but I can see myself painting in this shed. My own set of shelves brimming with paint cans, each one lovingly dripped in enamel shine. Sawhorses with a panel stretched across them, and lettering for Rancrest Farms mapped in pencil. It's not exciting work, but if I can't pull off my alternative signage show, it's good to keep my options open. I was so sure we'd break up today, but the possibilities here are softening my resolve.

In the shadows, John's arm is drooped over a scaffolding bar. "Taking this unit apart is going to be harder than I thought. One section is rusted tight."

I rise, brush floor dust off my pants and wave aside the metal beast. "Leave it here. You can use it for something else. A climber for your brothers, maybe. Let's go." I move for the door.

"Already? Let's stay a little longer." Quickly, John returns to me and his voice goes soft. He starts pivoting my hips toward him again, but I take his hand and lead him to the door. "That scaffolding?" I say as we move into the sunlight. I jerk my head in its direction. "It makes my brain dizzy."

"You and heights," John says.

"But the farm is impressive."

He brightens. "You think so?"

I scoop my arm under his. "I do," I say, which isn't supposed to sound so bride-and-groomy, but with any luck, John is too busy admiring his acreage to notice.

Chapter 15

A WEEK LATER, I STOP FOR A BITE to eat on the way to Velvet's.

"Small fries, Donny. No. Make that a medium." I wait on the weed-stomped patch of ground in front of his chipwagon and brush salt off the Arborite pass-through at the base of the window. I wouldn't mind if our local twenty-something French fryer jogged to the back field and dug up potatoes too. I'm in no rush to get to Velvet's. I've got lots of ideas for signs, and a few are even finished, but I'm less and less sure about posting them. The way people look at me—at the store or the grading station—I feel like everyone knows my dirty painting habit.

Donny's lanky skeleton is crammed into the trailer. Downy hair at the back of his head presses against the ceiling as he shakes the metal basket, hissing and spitting. "Got your cukes picked?" he calls out the half open window.

Putnam: Where Everyone Knows Your Business. I finished that sign a few days ago. "We're almost through. The grading station closes next week. Can I get vinegar?"

"Must be hard keeping up with the crop. Especially when you're busy with other things."

I stop with the salt cleaning.

Donny turns to face me and slides the window open the rest of the way. "You think that sign of mine needs a fresh coat?" He needles a bony finger out the window and jabs it upward.

I take two steps back. One step to move away from a possible accusation that I'm a sign painter, and another to politely check the title on his truck. I glance at the tired letters, cracked, black and painted by an inexperienced hand. "Looks fine to me. Not that I'm any kind of expert."

Donny rests his folded spindle arms on the counter of the pass-through. "Not an expert, huh? Not yet?" He grins like we're buddies.

Even Tammy Mills saw me biking to Velvet's the first time I visited. What was I thinking, making like I could paint a load of signs without anyone knowing?

"I hear you're quite the artist," he adds.

My throat closes up. "Nothing special." I keep the two step distance but I can see the fries turning golden. Pull my goddamn order out of the fryer, Donny Post.

He nods earnestly. "Good to have a dream, I always say."

"Sure. Those fries about ready?"

"Soon." Donny looks at me with a slightly crooked and knowing gaze.

I return my attention to the safety of his signage.

Finally he lets go of looking at me and checks my order. "Perfect," I hear him say. He lifts the basket from the fryer, shakes off the oil and pours a heap of crinkle-cuts into a paper bag. "You got extra," he adds, pushing the bag along the pass-through. "Good for an energy boost. Sounds like you might need it."

If Donny Post thinks he's on my side, I'll join a different team. I grab my fries.

"Vinegar?" He passes me a packet. I'd like ketchup too, but I don't want to extend the visit.

"Thanks." I drop the packet into the bag and swivel around like I've got an important appointment.

"Martha?"

What now? I stop. Warm grease soaks through the bag and onto my hand.

"Not sure if you know this, but I used to pass my days dreaming of race car driving." He leans against the pass-through with his elbow like he's getting comfortable for a long story. Maybe he just needs someone to talk to about his teenage days.

"I'd smoke another doob," he continues, "and flip through my three copies of *Road and Track*, so worn out the staples were missing and the pages all mixed up. I'd picture myself sitting behind the wheel and feel the speed. Nothing like having a dream," he adds, craning his head out more, "but trust me. Dreams can mess up your head. In the end, a guy has to uphold his responsibilities." He swirls a glance around the interior of his potato shrine.

Jesus McMurphy. I'm not sure if Donny's needling me about sign painting, or if he's passing wisdom to members of his imaginary union of vegetable processors. Either way, I'm out of here. "Sure, Donny. I should run."

"And Martha?"

Cripes.

"Working your ass off in a cucumber field isn't always fun, but it's what you agreed to do."

Donny is making me more uncomfortable than John's knee driving into my leg last week. The only thing I agreed to was a medium order of fries. I cram a fry into my mouth, wave goodbye and make a run for my bike and Velvet's place beyond.

As I careen down the highway, the decision about posting my paintings comes clear. Mounting a solo show would be suicide. Everyone would hate them. Hate me. Donny Post sent me a sign and I have to follow it.

IN VELVET'S CARPORT, the table is crowded with farm signs in various states of completion. The only space for me to work is on the floor, next to my half-eaten bag of fries. After I finish the deep shadows around the lettering, I tip up the board, drag it across the concrete and prop it against the wall. I sit on my haunches to view the effect. *Lonely Acres* is perfectly miserable, with letters the colour of a tired farmer's skin, and veering off to the edge until the last ones keel over and die.

I could die of boredom in Ridley Township, but I'll die of humiliation first if I post my signs.

"Finished already?" Velvet hustles into the carport, whomps her paisley gold photo album on the table and squats next to me. She nods at my latest. "Nice."

"It's for John's place."

"Oh? I thought the other sign was for him."

I glance uneasily at another painting in the corner, the one I made yesterday with his shed in mind: *Love Shack*, in hot pink letters that curve and bulge and press up against one other. I cover my eyes to block out the confusion. Rub them gently.

"Look. Both signs are the same size." Velvet springs up, grabs the *Love Shack* sign and wedges it next to *Lonely Acres*. "They belong together. Sweet and sour. The perfect combination."

I turn away from the signs. "Did you get the job for the hog farm?"

"Don't worry about me." Velvet glides to my stack of finished signs leaning against the wall and flips though them. "Do you need a sign for the other end of Putnam, too? Seems unfinished, having just one." She lifts out *Where Everyone Knows Your Business* and assesses it.

I stand up to meet her face to face. "I've been thinking, Velvet. Sticking signs along the side of the road for everyone to see is too risky. Just painting them—having them—is enough. I'll show the art colleges. That's all that matters."

"Opening night jitters?" she muses. Velvet returns the Putnam sign and pulls out another board. She props *Free Bullshit* against her hip and surveys it lovingly. "I'm especially fond of this one."

"The beef farmer won't be. That's what I'm talking about. He'll pitch a fit."

"He's a feisty one, but it's about time the truth came out."

"Velvet, I can't."

"Besides," she says, still gazing at the sign, "the lettering on this one is so vivid, so articulated and full of volume I can practically smell it."

"The signs aren't meant for everyone to see."

"They're just for you, are they?" A chill settles into Velvet's eyes.

"For us. You wanted me to voice truths in paint, as uncomfortable as they are. I'm doing that."

"I'm a proud sponsor of your exhibit." Velvet sets the *Bullshit* sign down and lifts a tin of paint. She holds it up like a fed up advertiser of cleaning products no one has the good sense to appreciate. "I've provided full use of exterior sign painting enamels. The wood and the use of my equipment."

"I've told you a hundred times. I'll pay for stuff. You keep saying no."

She moves in close, showdown style, her nostrils flaring. "But more important than supplies and equipment, which anyone can buy, I'm passing on hard-earned knowledge."

I lean back to spare myself the sight of the little hairs in her nostrils, heaving in and out.

"Finish the project, Martha. Mount the show."

I glance to the floor. "No one wants to see honest, meaningful messages. If they find out I'm the one who painted them, I'll be tortured."

Velvet's flaring nostrils calm to regular intervals. "Breathe, Martha. That's it. Full, healthy breaths. Anxiety is a poor condition for an artist. She must feel free and open, like a flowing river. Obstacles aren't good for you."

"Not good at all." I blow out air and set a lid on a paint tin.

"You're taking your place at the table of artists in Western history who pushed the boundaries. And as an added bonus, Putnam and area residents will see themselves in a truer, fresher light." Velvet pauses. "I wasn't going to tell you about the promotion underway."

I'm about to give the lid a smack, but I pause, my fist suspended.

"But it looks like I'll have to." Velvet leans against the table, suddenly relaxed. "You'll soon enjoy top publicity. The kind you get from showing your work to a highly influential member of the arts community. He's coming. He wants to view your work on display."

"Who?" I whack the lid.

"See? You're flustered already. If the pressure is too much, I can call him back. I'll say you're only interested in small potatoes art. Not exhibiting." She strokes her chin. "I guess there's nothing wrong with a life in Putnam. It's not like you wouldn't paint at all. Your dad can keep you busy making repros of old guy art."

"Who's coming, Velvet? Tell me." I level her a vicious look.

"Just someone well connected with the art world. Someone who can talk you up. Someone, incidentally, with a soft spot for text-based art."

"Text-based art?"

"Art that incorporates the written word."

I drop onto a stool. Text-based art. Where have I heard that word? I remember the newspaper review. I guess I belong to an art movement. Whoa.

"It's a rare opportunity. The guy is only best friends with the head of the painting department at the Royal Art College in Toronto." Velvet picks fluff off her shirt. "But I understand if you're too nervous to show him your work."

My golden ticket out of Putnam awaits. "You couldn't invite your friend to swing by the shop and check out the paintings here, could you?"

Velvet laughs low in her throat and folds her arms across her chest. "Context, baby. Install your pieces where they belong." She stares at me. "Show you're serious. Risky." Her eyebrows arch. "Daring."

I sit up tall, my eyes averted from *Lonely Acres* and *Love Shack*, and exhale. "I'll finish the project. I'll mount the signs." To hell with people's reactions.

Velvet's arms fall and she smiles big. "There's my *artiste* talking. Now that you're finished wringing your hands, let's nail down a date for the show." She moves to the Home Hardware calendar duct taped to the wall. "Not too far ahead. The reviewer has a busy schedule."

"He's writing a review?" Incredible.

"Hmm." Velvet nods and runs a finger down the month of August. "He's coming ... oh. Wow. This weekend already. Let's mount the signs Friday night. For a Saturday viewing."

"In four days?"

"You've made eight signs already. One more each day, and you'll have an even dozen. Perfect." Velvet smiles brightly. "I'll charge the cordless drill."

I try to ignore my insides caving in. "Friday night." I smile back, if you can call it that.

"Excited?" Velvet, her eyes dancing, digs in her drawer of power tools.

"Sure." I swallow and a sweat worse than the kind from late-morning cucumber picking drenches my chest.

Chapter 16

I SPOT THE FLASHLIGHT IN MY DESK DRAWER and slip it into the pocket of my sweater, dark green for roadside camouflage. Tonight I post the twelve signs. Proclaimers of all that is messed about Putnam. And tomorrow the big shot reviewer will see them. Not just see them, but probably love them and gush about me to his friend—his *best* friend—at the Royal Art College.

I arrange my hand over the bulge in my pocket and bounce downstairs. Wend my way around the scaffolding John erected in the middle of the house a few days ago. He went through two cans of WD-40 before he could take the thing apart, and surprised us the next day in the driveway. The truck he borrowed from home was loaded with metal parts. After John rebuilt the scaffolding in our house, I was too annoyed to thank him. He stomped off and drove away. We haven't spoken since, but I've had no time to iron out that problem.

"Don't be late," Velvet warned me. Nine p.m. Mom thinks I'm going to the drive-in with Bernie. Dad is out with Debbie, renting video equipment or something.

Mom, in the kitchen, scrapes the teakettle across the stove for her nighttime hit of chamomile.

"Don't wait up." I aim for a friendly but done deal assurance in my voice.

Mom pushes a droop of hair from her face. "Why don't you stay home tonight, Martha? You've been out so much." She sends a forlorn look to the network of steel zigzagging to the ceiling. "And you have to get that creation painting over with. I want the scaffolding out of here." Urgency mounts in her voice. "People are coming to see the film tomorrow night."

Dad and John shoved the dining/communion table against the wall to make room for the scaffolding. I haven't had trouble ignoring it. "I'll paint later, Mom. Bernie and I need a break from picking." I lean in to offer a cheek kiss.

She dribbles steaming water into her mug. "Dad's anxious for you to paint. Let's get the job done. Maybe the video idea will fly and..." Her voice trails off.

"And you can stop paying for his projects?"

Mom hesitates and looks away. "I wish we had more time to prepare for the screening. And I wish you'd just stay home."

"I'll give you a hand tomorrow." I check the clock on the stove. Yikes. Velvet said it's important to be punctual and professional. I zip to the front door and slide into my runners. Time to mount my One Girl Show of Bad Signs.

The door swishes open. "Hello, everyone!" Dad sings.

The flashlight tumbles out of my pocket.

"Sorry we're late," he adds.

I snatch up the light before it hits the floor.

"Well, hey there." From behind the video camera, Debbie points at my flashlight. "Going camping, Martha?"

I let it pass. I'll be like a ninja. A nighttime, slip-out-the-door ninja, quick and silent. After I lace up my runners.

"The plaza in Thorndale was open late," Dad says. "We bought supplies. Paint! Brushes!" He's carrying two gallons of paint in one hand, and in the other, a plastic bag that he rattles like jingle bells.

"Oh, yeah?" I make an effort to look distracted, like I'm already long gone. It's just my shoelaces holding me back.

"Where are you going, Martha?" Concern deepens Dad's voice. He sets down the bags.

"To the drive-in with Bernie." I stand tall. Glide a hand to the aluminum panel of door and nudge it open. The hinge creaks.

Dad clamps onto the door handle. "Tonight?"

"Sure." I shrug and smile. The evening's itinerary isn't usual, but I have to make it sound that way.

Mom trudges out from the kitchen. "I told her to stay home, but she wouldn't listen."

My toe searches out the slim strip of fresh, night air between the door and the frame.

"Martha," Dad barks, like I've wandered onto a highway of speeding traffic.

I pull back.

"Tonight's our big night." He shifts to a manic smile and practically thunders, Godlike, "Tonight we paint the *Creation of Adam!*"

"But I promised Bernie." My chest thumps. It's *my* big night, not his. Terror, that's what it is. Fear of entrapment.

"Go another night. The scaffolding is waiting, the paints are ready and Debbie—Debbie?"

"Uh-huh?" Debbie, droid-like, lowers the camera.

"Debbie is set to record."

God help me.

"It's a rental," she says. "We have to return it Monday, but we want to film a 'making of the video' part. I'm recording all the steps. I'll tape you painting, okay Martha?"

"I can't paint tonight."

"Nuh-uh." Dad holds a shushing finger to his lips. "'Can't' isn't a word at the Becker Institute. I'll call Bernie. Explain that you have pressing business at home."

"No, Dad." My blood starts boiling worse than Mom's tea-kettle.

Dad waltzes to his desk, presses the phone receiver to his chest and calls back, "I'll take responsibility for this one."

"Don't! I'll do it." I start after him.

"Shoes, Martha! Not in the house," Mom says, and in the moment of hesitation when my soles freeze on the hardwood floor, Dad flops the address book open and starts pushing numbers. I watch in frozen fear as each number drags him closer to Bernie's ignorance about the movie I said we'd see tonight.

As Dad chatters into the phone, I pull off my shoes and limp to the scaffolding, grasp an upright pole and rest my head against it. I can say anything I want on a sign, but inside this house, I'm helpless. Now my show is ruined. My golden ticket out of Putnam, gone. I thump my head against the pole and try not to cry.

"Good news, Martha," Dad says, cheerfully clattering the phone back in its cradle. "Bernie didn't know about a movie. You must have had the wrong night."

I slump, my insides avalanching into a pit of despair.

"Wrong night?" Mom says, sipping tea. "That's peculiar."

I avoid her gaze; keep my distance from brewing suspicions. I do look at the clock. Nine-thirty. God.

"I wonder if we bought too much paint." Debbie takes the gallons from Dad and hauls them over to me. Both have dabs of Pepto-Bismol pink on their lids. "This is skin colour, by the way."

"It's good to have extra," Dad says.

"True," Debbie agrees. "In case she makes a mistake."

I could mistake a gallon of paint across her head.

"Up you go, Martha," Dad says, grinning wildly. "I'll aim the floodlights so you can see what you're doing."

I bet Michelangelo never had this kind of pressure. But there's no time for tears or protests or throwing myself on the floor in a flurry of thrashing appendages. I have to paint like hell. Create Adam all over again so that after Debbie leaves and Dad starts snoring, I can sneak out the door and mount my signs, if Velvet isn't too pissed at me for waking her up in the middle of the night to help.

"I'm not going to spend a long time at this," I warn them all.

"She's staying," Mom whispers gratefully, and mumbles *adieu* to the scaffolding.

"You'll be finished in no time." Dad beams. "I'll tell you what. Just paint God's outstretched hand alighting Adam's finger."

"Not the little naked bits," Debbie adds, her nose wrinkling.

"No," Dad agrees. "Only the all important detail. The moment when all things are possible. When success and achievement are imminent."

I groan and haul my bare foot onto the bottom stair of scaffolding.

"She's doing it!" Debbie swings her lens in my direction. "I missed your first step, Martha. Start over, okay? Ready? And … action!"

DEBBIE TOLD ME HER JUNIOR HIGH ART TEACHER thinks drawing hands is the hardest part of figure work. I drag pinkness over God's fingernail. Two coats. Scratch behind my ear with the end of the paintbrush. Three. I'm considering a solitary, monk-like existence atop this steel-barred mountain. Passing years or even decades smoothing God's arthritic, gnarled and grossly oversized mitt.

A sliver of moon hangs beyond the arched window. I'm working in slo-mo.

So tired. At ceiling altitude, the air feels like rotting compost heat. Thick, heavy and tinged with the bite of paint fumes. Camera girl turned off the recorder and went home.

A few hours ago, Debbie made me open the paint can a second time, and smile. Just once more. From the top!

I adjust my safety belt—formerly Dad's flannel plaid bathrobe tie—that leashes me to a metal bar of scaffolding. After I finish God's fingernails, I slump on the plywood floor to rest my arms. Straining up uses different muscles than the ones for reaching down to pick cucumbers, for example. Or paint signs in a carport.

My signs.

I curl up on the wooden floor and remember Velvet's phone call an hour ago. The phone cord wouldn't reach the ceiling. Dad asked her if she was the one who was supposed to go to the drive-in with me. He didn't sound happy or positive. After a long pause, he said, "Martha isn't interested in sign painting projects right now. She's applying her efforts to more noble pursuits."

Before he returned to his desk, Dad cheered me on to stay true to the Becker Institute, and reminded me about steering clear of the competition.

I imagined myself an angry pigeon looking down on Dad—on his thin whorl of brownish grey hair hovering over his desk. I slid the loaded brush beyond my elevated enclosure and tapped the side of the brush, like a smoker knocking off cigarette ash. The fat drop of pinkness clung to the bristles for a moment and then let go. Down. Down. But the faux bird do missed its hairy target, and unbeknownst to Dad, splatted in the wicker garbage pail beside his desk.

I can't paint anything.

After a few more hours of painting, the-man-on-whom-no-dripped-paint-can-fall is asleep on the couch near the front door. Drugged by paint fumes, I decide to sleep for a minute or two, but no more. My eyelids weaken. I'll sneak by the guard. Later. I'll mount my signs. I keep my promises.

I sink to the plywood flooring, tuck in my knees and curl into a pink paint spattered ball.

Chapter 17

"MARTHA. COME DOWN." The voice is distant and small.

Morning sun streams through the window and dust particles swarm in its rays. I twist and shift, driving my hip into something stiff and unyielding. What in hell? My mattress feels as hard as a gangplank.

I remember where I am and unfurl my legs. Look down. Way down.

A paint fume hangover drags on my head.

My art show.

My once-in-a-lifetime opportunity to be reviewed and connected with the head of the painting department at the Royal Art College. Gone.

My future.

I roll onto my back and stare at God, reaching down to crush me.

"Have a fried egg, Martha," Mom calls up.

I groan at God the Father, another dad lording over me.

"It's not a bad painting," the dad downstairs adds, morning enthusiasm fueling his tone. "It captures a tension not existent in the original."

A sharp rapping at the front door interrupts him.

I sit up. Or try to, but Dad's bathrobe belt squeezes my waist. "Come in," he calls.

I peek over the edge of scaffolding. The door opens.

"Leanne," Dad says, ushering her inside. "Have I got a painting to show you."

Leanne's ever-curled hair shines and sways in the front hall. Reliably superficial Leanne, come to rescue me.

"Is Martha home?"

"Up here," I call.

Leanne gurgles surprise, and her eyes swim up the zagging stairs of scaffolding. They land on my poking-up head at the top. "Holy sh—"

"Look way up. At the ceiling," Dad says, pointing.

Her gaze scales the full height of our church interior and stops on my Abomination of Adam, dried to a darker hue than I remember from last night. "Hey." She parks her hands on her hips and cocks her upturned head. "I think I've seen a picture like that before."

"*The Creation of Adam*," Dad says, clapping elated hands together. "See Peggy? I knew people would recognize it. I'm so glad you've come, Leanne. Did you hear that, Martha?" he calls. "Leanne knows the painting!"

Leanne's sightline returns to ground level. "I was driving by. I wondered if Martha wanted to come out. I'm heading to Thorndale, to the diner for coffee."

I pick at the knot on the flannel belt. Must get out of here. Away from the fumes and the hand of God.

"Sorry, Leanne," Dad says. "Martha's extremely tired."

"I'm awake," I say from the top of the scaffolding.

"Maybe it's best if she's out," Mom says. "Debbie is coming soon. The house will have to be silent." For the filming, Mom means. Debbie has to tape Dad's one hour seminar with the *Creation of Adam* above him. For once I'm glad she's coming.

"Right," Dad murmurs. "Martha!" he yells. "How would you like to join your friend for the rest of the morning?"

"Coming," I call. The knot comes loose and I shrug the plaid lasso down my hips. If it weren't for the wide abyss between the scaffolding and my bedroom loft, I could leap into my room to change. I keep hold of the rail as I descend the metal steps. My knees wobble inside yesterday's clothes, wrinkled and smudged.

Leanne grins up at me. "Tough night, Martha?"

As my parents peer at the ceiling atrocity, I give her the finger.

"Tammy's waiting in the car," she says. "I've got so much to tell you. You'll never believe who I met today."

I take careful steps down the final flight of stairs to the comfort of mildly irritating friends and their gossip. If only Leanne knew who I *didn't* meet.

LEANNE REACHES INTO THE BACK SEAT and shakes me awake. Groggily, I lift my head off the side window. Must've slept the last twenty minutes. Past the glaring sun, the sign for the Sunset Diner settles into focus. I look away. Any sign brings an aching sense of loss.

"Come on, Martha," says Tammy Mills from the front seat. "Leanne won't tell the rest of the hot-guy story until you're awake."

If only I could block out signs forever. Sleep away the rest of my life. My eyelids lower. Shut. A headache still presses into the sides of my skull.

"Wake up, Martha," Tammy Mills says. "Leanne drove all the way back to Putnam to get us."

I push the car door open and heave my legs onto the sidewalk. The three of us, with me trailing behind, chime through the diner door and take our regular spot near the back.

"I'll start all over," Leanne says with a sigh. She passes out the vinyl, padded menus she scooped up on the way in. "So this morning. I'm on breakfast, and this guy comes into the diner. Never seen him before. Twenty-five, maybe. He's got soft, golden hair down to his shoulders and he's wearing a sweater like his mom made it. And she's a kick-ass knitter. Goes all out for alpaca. Doesn't mind having fun with stripes, either."

"The jeans,'" Tammy Mills says, flipping open her menu. "Talk about his jeans again."

Leanne sinks lower in her bench seat. "It's like they were professionally faded to accentuate his muscles." Luxuriously, she eases her hands down her thighs.

Tammy Mills bounces a look between us and smiles.

I prop up my head with my hand. "Who're you talking about?" I mumble.

"Just listen," Leanne says. "The guy is researching—get this— the *local artwork*."

A funny kind of tickle stirs at the back of my neck. "What kind of artwork?"

Leanne jerks a thumb to the pictures hanging on the wall— the local artists' landscapes painted off postcards from some Caribbean island or the Rocky Mountains. "I figure he means these ones, so I show him."

The tickle flickers away. I lean against the wall and avert my sightline from the string of storefront signs across the street.

"I figure the paintings are why he's hauled his cute ass all the way from Toronto," Leanne goes on. "But the guy glances at them and turns his head, disgusted. 'Not those,' he says. He's got to be from Toronto, with the fake California accent."

Oh, God. Maybe it *is* the guy Velvet invited, all the way from the city to see a road full of nothing.

Tammy Mills twists around to reassess the parade of paintings on the wall. "Maybe he doesn't know nothing about art."

"Anyway," Leanne says, "he suddenly apologizes for not 'taking the time to introduce himself.'"

Tammy Mills sticks her pinky out and bats her lashes. "He a fancy guy?"

"Sophisticated," Leanne explains. "Tall and lean, too."

"Not Bernie's type of guy," I add. It just slips out from my sleepy stupor.

"What do you mean?" Tammy Mills asks.

"She likes heft in her men." Oops. Wasn't supposed to mention that either.

"She told you that?" Leanne looks slightly annoyed, like the Bernie detail is a distraction from her story. "Anyway, the guy says he's working for a magazine. *Arts* something. I forget the name, but he drops it like everyone should know. He's looking for outsider art. Art done outdoors, I guess he meant. Blaa blaa, until finally he mentions—ready? The signs. The signs! Can you believe it?"

I jerk to life. Sit tall. "What signs?"

Tammy Mills looks at me like I'm an idiot. "If you stayed awake, you'd have seen them on the way here. Somebody painted a bunch of goofball signs. Poked them into the ditch up and down Putnam Road." She leans into her opened menu.

My twelve signs! Velvet put them up after all! Or maybe God Himself, after he was done creating Adam and I fell asleep, floated down from the ceiling and brought my art show to life! "The reporter guy wants to write about the signs?" I ask a little too hungrily.

"Not that they're *art*," Tammy Mills says, rolling her eyes.

"But they're what the reporter guy is looking for," Leanne says, back to her story. "He got a tip from a friend. He says he's also interested in 'text-based' stuff."

"Text-based." I try not to swoon. "I love that idea."

"Doesn't mean nothing at all," Tammy Mills says, like I'm in kindergarten. But I don't care because the signs are up, and the word will get back to the head of the painting department at the Royal Art College. I sit on my hands to keep them from flapping up and down in a flurry of excitement.

"So Hot Pants buys a coffee and asks if I could direct him to one of the 'pieces,'" Leanne says. "Well, honey, let *me* show you a piece of art." She stretches back, pulling her already tight shirt taut across her twin glories.

"You didn't really say that, did you?" Tammy Mills asks, her shoulders squeezed up hopefully.

"I *think* it," Leanne says. "I tell him I'm off work in a few minutes. That I'm going home by way of the signs and he can follow me."

I hope he likes them. I hope, I hope, I hope.

"And?" Tammy Mills says.

"He's driving behind me, and we pull up to the sign for Putnam, the one whining how it's too gossipy—that's a piece of work—and I figure he's going to either laugh his head off or act disgusted like he did with the landscapes." Leanne pauses to check for our waitress.

"I like the ocean scene best, with the pink seashells," Tammy Mills says.

"But no. The guy pulls over," Leanne says, "walks straight up to the first sign and makes little happy noises at the back of his throat. He likes it."

I hide my freewheeling smile behind my napkin, although it's probably peeking out from my eyes.

"Was he a little…?" Tammy Mills taps her temple as though she can make the marbles fall out.

"No, Tammy," Leanne says. "He's from Toronto. They *like* weird shit there. But by this point I'm wondering if his brain is so packed with artsy thoughts that he doesn't have room to think about girls." She stretches and arches her back.

I don't even know this guy—my angel, my messenger, proclaiming to the world the glories of text-based art—but already I want to protect him from Leanne's pushy chest.

"Then he spots another sign, *False Dreams*, or something out near Martha's house and sprints up to it. Doesn't even care about dragging the bottoms of his jeans through the weeds." She shakes her head. "I start walking away, because I have stuff to do. It's my time off, don't forget."

"And?" Tammy Mills asks.

"He comes back blabbing about the signs being a reaction against conformity. Comments on rural conservative thinking. Something like that. He has all kinds of crap to dish out before he starts into more questions."

"Like?" I ask.

"Like how have people in the area embraced the pieces?"

"The signs would have been yanked out already if Robbie Nieman hadn't of gone on holidays," Tammy Mills says.

"Ronnie Nieman?" I ask.

"You know," Tammy Mills says. "The maintenance guy for the township. Him and his wife went to Sault Ste. Marie to visit her parents. The signs have to annoy people for another week until they get back."

"Where in hell is Lorna? The service stinks in here," Leanne says.

A week of glory. I could sprint to the bathroom, lock the stall door, and in my mind whoop and holler silent cheers.

"But here's the real news, guys," Leanne says, her voice lowering. "Hot Pants gets my phone number."

"Whoa." Tammy Mills closes her menu solemnly.

"In case he has more questions about the paintings, he *says*." Leanne slides a bounce of blonde behind her ear and lowers her voice. "But actually? I think he's interested in yours truly. He just can't handle me while he's working." A cat smile spreads across her face.

Tammy Mills nods. "Wow. City boy."

"Oh," Leanne adds, returning to regular volume. "My new friend also wants to know if the artist is known or remaining anonymous."

The cheers in my head disappear.

"I'd like to know who painted them things," Tammy Mills says. "That sign painter, maybe. Velvet Rudder. I bet she did them. Or the Doyle boys. They spray-painted graffiti on the dumpster out back of Forbes Manufacturing."

"Except they can't spell," Leanne says. "Remember? They wrote *Satin Rules* instead of *Satan Rules*."

"Then it's Velvet," Tammy Mills says, looking to me.

"Naw." I wish I could rig up a muffler to my heart, clanging and hammering. "She's got a business to run. She wouldn't have time for all that."

"Then who?" Tammy Mills says.

"So Putnam's in the news," I say real quick. "Because of some signs."

"Not real news. Not like the *Toronto Star*," Leanne says. "Just for some art magazine no one's heard of."

Just then, Leanne's fellow waitress shuffles to our table, presses her peach lacquered fingertips on the Arborite and leans over. "Hey, girls. Sorry it's taken me so long. This place is nuts. You know those sign things around Putnam? People are getting real pissed about them."

"Which people?" Tammy Mills says.

"You know the Schellenbergers?" Lorna asks.

"Bernie's our neighbour," Leanne says.

"Her dad was in Home Hardware this morning talking to the boys. He was ready to boil over."

The headache, lying in wait in the basement of my brain, marches up to my forehead and pounds its fists.

"By the new sign for his chicken farm," Lorna carries on, "somebody put up, *but she likes them beefy*. Right underneath Bernie's name."

"We didn't see that one," Tammy Mills says, locking eyes with Leanne.

"We were driving the other way," Leanne says.

I sink lower on the bench as the pounding grows.

Lorna's forehead pinches up. "Whoever painted those signs knows the particulars of Bernie Schellenberger."

"Her manly interests." Tammy Mills stares at Leanne. I bet their brain waves are tumbling over each other and twisting into a rushing vortex.

Leanne and Tammy Mills swing their sets of eyes toward me and bring them in for a hard landing. The other adrenalin courses through me—the flight one. But the diner's rear exit is blocked by five-gallon pails of margarine. The front door is swarming with regular Thorndale cronies. It's just a matter of time before someone who I dissed in a sign appears. I've painted my own nightmare.

I steal another look to the front door.

A miracle occurs; one no smaller than Jesus's stroll upon water. John MacIntosh walks into the diner.

"Hey." My voice croaks as I stand up. John has been snubbing me since he brought the scaffolding over, but maybe he'll feel like talking today.

"Wait," Tammy Mills says.

"Gotta say hi. John!" I slip out from the seat, stumble over a table leg and prance to the door, away from the stares burning into my back.

When I reach the cash, John looks at me like I'm a stranger. A weird one. Stoned or loopy. Not suitable for respectable people in John Deere caps like himself.

I shove the hurt aside and aim for cheerful. "Hey. That scaffolding works real good. You should come over. Check out our new ceiling," I say with a light laugh and double sugar in my voice.

"Came in for a coffee." Without looking at me, he nods thanks to the girl at the cash, sips from his take-out, and turns for the door.

"What's the big rush?" Desperately, I tail him out of the diner and along the sidewalk. I cringe when the owner of Binscarth's Auto Body walks toward us. He did such a bad job on Velvet's truck, I signed him too. Painted *Auto get a job I can do properly* for his garage. I bet Velvet put that one up for sure.

The diner door chimes behind us. I'll bet it's Leanne and Tammy, wielding menus and shaking them. I pick up the pace. Keep my gaze on the sidewalk as Velvet's neighbour passes by. "Feel like going for a drive?" I ask John.

"Need a lift, do you?" When he stops at his parked blue Datsun, regret for its matching vinyl interior sweeps over me. Nostalgia for a simpler time a few weeks ago, when I just wanted to get laid for the first time.

"She's getting away." Leanne is behind me, louder and closer.

"I do need a lift, John. Please?" I dart a look back at Leanne and Tammy Mills—at the pinpoints of Leanne's eyes.

"Aw, geeze, Martha," John says, in such a hurry he doesn't seem to notice my pursuers. "I haven't got time."

He didn't say no, so I swing his door open and jump in. "I just want to go home."

His engine roars to life. "I'm heading for the farm in Ridley." He sighs as he backs up. "I'll drop you off on the way."

I lock the door and fix my gaze ahead. "Gun it, John." I brace myself for Leanne and Tammy Mills's shouts or fists thundering on the trunk before John can get me the hell out of here.

Chapter 18

THORNDALE SINKS AWAY as John's Datsun motors up to highway speed and the shocked faces of Leanne and Tammy Mills grow smaller in my side mirror. I take calming breaths and wonder if John has seen the signs. If he knows they're mine. Oh, God. I rest my head against the side window as cornfields sweep past my window.

I thought my signs would float through local lore and disappear, an oddity with no one to credit or blame, like the night the mailboxes disappeared off their posts, or the time the McCowan's Volkswagen Beetle mysteriously wound up on the roof of their addition. Only my signs would be more than a prank or petty crime. They'd hold truths. Honest, revealing messages some people might even understand. And outside Putnam, the messages would stir interest at an art college.

John shoves the gearshift into fifth. We drive in silence. I wonder if my parents have seen the signs. My gut squeezes tight.

Up ahead, a dark blur appears—a foreign object on Highway 7. I yank my head off the window. My sign. Standing tall and facing oncoming traffic.

John jabs his thumb toward the blur. "I'm surprised no one's ripped those things down yet. Who'd you abuse on that one?"

I freeze. The blur materializes into a sign reaching up from the grassy ditch like a kid in class with his hand stuck in the air, desperate for attention. I shrink down as the letters take shape. *Putnam: Where Everyone Knows Your Business.*

"Had to start out thumbing your nose at the entire village first off, huh Martha? In case you missed someone in particular later on?"

"I didn't…" Aw, hell. He knows. Everyone knows.

"People are taking the words to heart," I say, suddenly exhausted. "More than I expected."

"I knew it," he says. "I knew Velvet would take you on some crazy trip."

Near the turn-off to Lowe's grading station, *No Nubs and Crooks Allowed* appears. I perk up a little at the deliberately mis-shapen letters, barbed with prickles and edged in spent orange blossoms. The sign is well crafted. Not that anyone will care.

Free Bullshit follows, stuck in a lawn by the mailbox. Velvet's favourite sign.

"That man is running for county reeve next election," John says, his teeth set together.

"He never stops talking."

"You don't have the right, Martha." Frustration bites into his voice.

At Doreen's, we pass *Superiority Farms, Where We Think We're Better than You.* Velvet remembered to post the sign higher than the rest so it peers at drivers below. The sign looks bigger than I remembered. Nastier. Darker.

"You slandered your own sister." John shakes his head. "Unbelievable."

As we pass under Doreen's sign glaring down in its sharp script, my insides start crumbling. We pass Bernie's farm and

I slump against the side window. Next to Velvet's respectable marker, *Schellenberger Farms, Norm, Barb and Bernadette*, my sign is crammed below Bernie's name: *But She Likes Them Beefy.*

I rub my forehead. "I didn't think … oh, God."

John slows as we pass through the village, past the store with the Lottario sign in the window and *Be a Loser, You'll Fit Right In* crammed alongside. Next to the store's front door, at the shop where the owner gives you an earful, *Ask about Our Cheap Sex Jokes* is cocked at a mad angle. I could crawl under John's rubber floor mat and hide underfoot forever.

"Why'd you paint all that stuff?" he asks. He can't keep out the sneer. "Why'd you have to make everyone feel so miserable inside?"

"I was just trying my voice," I say, and swallow.

"What did people ever do to you?"

"I didn't set out to hurt anyone."

"*Lonely Acres,* huh?" His shoulders stiffen. "I saw that one, too."

I skip a breath. "I'm sorry, John. Really. I wasn't thinking about how it would sound."

"And *Love Shack.*" He checks his rear view. "I pulled over for a close up and noticed a spaceship drifting away from the corner."

"It wasn't like I was making fun of all that. I'm not a big sci-fi fan and that's the truth, but I'm glad you write stories. For you."

John doesn't say anything. He doesn't seem in the mood for encouragement.

I stare through the window as we approach our house and *False Dreams, Turn Right*, with its cloud-puffy, bloated letters.

John sighs. "As irritating as your Dad can be, I feel sorry for the guy. His sign is worse than *Lonely Acres.*"

"Maybe Mom and Dad haven't seen the signs. They've been cooped up inside, getting the film ready for the screening tonight."

For the first time today, John looks at me. Then his eyes return to the road and he shakes his head. "Your Dad's going to … well. I don't even want to think about it." He gears down before our house.

"What am I going to do?" I grip the door handle.

"Your dad believed in you," John adds, more to himself. He turns into our driveway and parks behind Dad's car.

"You don't want to come in, do you?"

"No." He switches the steering wheel to the other hand and sits tall. "I'm heading to the farm. Today's the day I take possession."

"Really?" If I weren't so piss-in-my-pants scared of getting slaughtered by my parents, I'd have room to feel truly happy for him.

"I might stop by later, though."

"Oh, yeah?" I pull away from the window. Maybe John will stand by me after all. Cover me when Dad explodes.

"To pick up the scaffolding," he adds. "I've got roofing to start on."

"Oh." I stare at our front door.

"*Lonely Acres*," John repeats, gazing at the clouds. "It's going to be all mine." He raps on the steering wheel. "Anyway. I have to go, and you need to get things over with."

I creak open the car door. Dad could be standing in the front hall right now. Waiting. "You're sure you don't want to come in?"

John pushes the gearshift into reverse. "You'll be fine, Martha." He coughs. "You go on now."

Chapter 19

THE HOUSE IS SILENT. I search past the network of scaffolding. Mom and Dad are huddled over the computer at Dad's desk. Debbie must have come and gone already. I slip my shoulder bag off and set it on the baptismal font. I'm safe. For the moment, anyway.

Dad is leaning back with his eyes shut like he's in deep meditation. His voice purrs from the speakers: "After this seminar, you'll walk away surer of your chances for success both at home and in the workplace."

Mom clicks off the voice.

"Hi," I say. My voice quivers.

"Let's keep the rousing music first and then splice in the introduction," Dad says to her, like I never arrived. They know. They know about the signs and they're shunning me.

"I tried that already. You didn't like it," Mom says, her voice strained. "Just leave it, Gerald. We've left the editing too late."

Or maybe they're finishing the video first, and plan to deal with why in God's name their daughter defiled the neighbourhood later. Either way, I sense a window of opportunity. Just a crack of one.

"Hi," I try again. "I might head out for a bike ride." Might just pull down those signs while I can.

"Martha." Dad's eyes bolt open. "I'm so glad you're home!" He claps his hands together, jumps up and sprints toward me. I tense my knees and grab the door handle. His enthusiasm must be a cover. "Fortunately, we have an extra gallon of pink," he continues, pausing at the scaffolding and pointing a finger upward. "Your mom thought you'd still have time to paint over the *Creation of Adam* before the screening tonight."

Mom glances up from her work. "We're not sure if Renaissance painting is your style exactly. Would you mind, Martha? While the scaffolding is still up?" She smiles in weak apology.

Maybe they haven't found out about the signs after all. I crane my neck and peer at God giving me the thumbs down. This morning I thought he looked like he'd suffered a nasty ski accident, but now I wonder if he's sending me a message to give up painting.

"Repainting shouldn't take long," Mom adds, her attention back on the video.

"I saw a roller in the storage room. I can get it if you'd like," Dad offers.

I pull shut the front door. Block out the outdoors and slip off my shoes. Given my current delicate position in the neighbourhood, I decide to be as co-operative as possible. "I don't think I'm a Renaissance painter either," I say. I'll whitewash God and Adam as quick as possible. Then I'll pull down those signs. "I'll find the roller myself."

LATER, I CLIMB ON MY TEN SPEED. Time to hit the highway and visit Velvet. Painting the ceiling took longer than I thought, but obliterating the creation story got me thinking how important it is that I pull down the goddamn signs. They weren't messages of creation at all. They were nothing but destructive. I'll use Velvet's pick-up truck, with or without her help. Fling the signs in the back and dump them in her yard—in the barbecue pit with the little painted stones around it. Light a long match and watch them burn.

Dad's positive thinking video premieres tonight at eight, free to all and taking place in our home. Unless I do something quick, everyone who comes will see the *False Hopes, Turn Right* sign and all the other painted nasties blighting the road to the Becker Institute.

I pedal hard and scan for my first painted nightmare along the grassy ditch.

I brake on the gravel. The sign should be standing by the tilted fence post. I study the silent, waving grass, but where *False Hopes* should be, there's only trampled weeds and a muddy hole. A welt in the earth.

The sign is gone. My heart convulses. I climb back on my bike and race along the edge of the highway, but the next sign is gone too, and the one after that. They've all disappeared leaving only holes in their places. Maybe the township authorities seized the signs for evidence in court, in the case against Martha Becker, the accused.

The charge, your honour?

I pedal harder.

Paint crime.

Gravel crunches under my wheels as I pedal past another gape in the earth. As horrid as those signs were, they were all I had left.

Even God has disappeared off the ceiling.

Velvet's place is another mile away, but inside my head, I'm already calling her name.

I DROP MY BIKE ON THE GRASS and sprint to her carport. "Velvet!"

The air in the paint shop hangs mute and empty. Her walls, once jumbled with signs in various states of completion, are vacant. Only ghosts of signs remain—wisps that mark the over-painted edges of ovals and rectangles. My knees go weak.

I yank open the wobbly drawer of her table. Her blue order book is gone. The paisley gold photo album, too.

I jog to the house and bang on the door. Ring the bell with the painted arrow pointing to it. Twice, in case the first time didn't work. "Velvet!" I yell through the smudged glass.

A sparrow twitters in the distance—a stupid brainless bird that sweeps overhead every day but can't tell me a damn thing about Velvet Rudder's whereabouts.

"Velvet!" I yell, louder.

I wrench on the doorknob. Surprisingly, it turns, and I swing the door open to a silent kitchen. A few mugs remain in the sink. A bulging garbage bag sags on the floor with an empty jam jar toppled alongside it. Two ripped vinyl chairs are stacked in the corner, but the room is otherwise empty.

Velvet couldn't have left without telling me.

Her walls are painted in gigantic Spirographs of colour that look like a map of her spinning mind. I lose myself inside a whirl of red splashed on her wall in gutsy, looping geometry. A footstep breaks the silence. A weighty, man-heavy one. With a warning bell clanging in my head—I'm trespassing, after all—I twist around.

"If ya've come to clean out the crap," the man says, "by all means." He'd be a nub if he were a cucumber, squat and bulbous—prickly too, around his jawline anyway.

I remember to exhale. "I'm a friend of Velvet's." I hope my voice doesn't sound too needy. "I'm not sure what happened to her."

"Couldn't pay rent is what happened." He's chomping gum.

"Velvet? She didn't tell me anything." I stop before I accidentally betray her. Velvet could've been working paying jobs, but she was too busy helping me realize my idiotic dreams. "I didn't know." My voice feels hollow. I turn to the man. "Who are you? Her landlord?"

He totters to the sink, lifts the plastic mugs out and glances at the garbage bag on the floor. "'Fraid so."

The man dumps the mugs into the garbage. "You're her friend, are ya?"

"I am, and I can help you clean up." I grab a broom from against the wall and start swishing the floor. Anything to get information on Velvet.

"Grab them chairs, too."

"Did she say where she was going?"

Velvet's landlord snorts as he creaks himself over the garbage bag to tie up the corners. "I seen her a little while ago, uprooting one of them godawful signs along Highway 7."

I give the broom a rest. My signs aren't being used as court evidence after all.

"Didn't have no rent on her, no surprise, but she was all loony-excited about selling them signs in the city."

"She's selling them?" Velvet must have wanted to surprise me. Dad was right after all. Believe in yourself and success will follow.

The man yanks the knot tight. "Said she'd pay me fair 'n' square after the signs sold. Even had a buyer." He scoffs.

Excitement sparkles up the back of my neck.

The man's eyes go slitty and dark. "I says to her, 'You always got a sale around the corner.' Doesn't matter, anyhow. She found herself someone else to mooch off."

"Who?"

The man stares at me hard for a second. "For a friend, you don't know much."

I twist the hairs at the back of my neck. "I know Velvet more professionally."

His eyebrows bunch up. "You a painter, too?"

"I am."

"But you don't know that guy she's hooked up with."

"What guy?"

"Dapper sorta dresser?" the man offers.

I skip a beat. "The arts reporter?"

He shrugs.

"Was he wearing a hand-knit sweater?" Frantically, I scroll through my memory for Leanne's description. "With stripes? Alpaca wool?" I skip the sculpted thigh detail.

"I wouldn't know. But lover boy was sitting in his four cylinder coupe along the side of the road while she did the heavy work yanking out signs.

"Lover boy?"

"Boyfriend, whatever you want to call him. That's what I figure. Anyway, this one didn't look like he gets his nails dirty. Finally hauled himself out of his vehicle and says to me, 'Do you have some sort of problem, sir?' And I says, 'I certainly do. This girl owes me four months back rent.'"

Velvet's complaints about piled bills and rent notices echo in my mind.

"The guy disappears into his car, comes out with his chequebook and pays me every last cent." He drags a look across the room. "'Cept she left me all this."

"Did she say anything about the buyer for the paintings?" A famous gallery, maybe.

"Said something about a collector in Toronto." He snorts. "Can't imagine folks in the city'd appreciate that brand of humour. Drag them chairs out to the truck, will ya? I'll take them to the dump."

My signs are being sold to a collector! Velvet is a twentieth century goddess. I lift a chair and float toward the door.

"Lord knows why," he adds, "but she was proud of them things. Said painting them signs was some kinda new beginning for her."

I drop the chair with a thud. "She said *she* painted the signs?"

"She's the sign painter." The man creaks the door open.

For an endless moment I stall, my hands hovering over the dropped chair. I could take the perfect escape route from sign painting ownership. Agree that Velvet painted them. That's my story, I'll tell everyone. I'll be free of all the anger coming at me. But a feeling bigger and fiercer gets in the way. I level Velvet's ex-landlord a ferocious look and knock the chair aside. "Those paintings are mine."

His lips go into hiding as he swallows a smirk. "They are, are they? Well, now. Isn't that something?"

A new wave of disdain washes over the guy's eyes and I shrink back a step or two. "Yeah. Velvet ... uh ... gave me the paintings." I cough into my fist. I wanted to claim the paintings as my own work, but I can't. Not now, with a surly guy glaring at me. "As a going-away gift. For her going-away, that is." I veer toward the door, trip on the chair and stumble out of the house. Each step awakens in me the sick truth about Velvet. Goddess, my ass. Velvet Rudder is nothing but a lying, thieving paint shark who left me nothing but a bad reputation.

AN HOUR LATER, I'm leaning against the blanket box at the end of my bed and doodling a fierce swirl on an old binder. Honesty in art, Velvet would go on about. I jab the pen at the binder until the plastic rips.

"I still wish we had a strong visual for the beginning of the film," I hear Dad say downstairs. "I'm just a talking head. We have no pictures."

Mom's shaky voice jangles up to my loft. "It's too late now, Gerald." She's probably dusting the pipe organ or baptismal font or altar, or switching nervously among them all. "People are coming any minute."

The phone rings. I've been reluctantly taking calls all day. After the eighth caller screamed in my ear, I settled on a new tactic. I snatch the receiver before the second ring. "Hello." I aim for masculine and slow, a voice I invented with Leanne for prank calls when we were nine.

"Is Martha Becker there?" It's a stranger. Not a friendly one.

"Wrong number." I hang up.

"Martha?" Dad calls up. "Who was that?"

"Bernie. She can't come to the screening. She's not feeling well." I've lost track of the calls. Mostly they're strangers with badly disguised scorn, hungry for the sordid details of my signage show. Few friends and neighbours want to chat.

"Then who *is* coming?"

I drag myself off the floor and lean over the edge of the loft. "Debbie," I begin.

"And?" Dad adjusts the angle of the projector screen downstairs. Its prim triangle of legs teeters precariously and settles back to the floor.

"John."

Mom and Dad look up from the rows of pews they've arranged for viewers. The dismantled scaffolding is outside, leaning against the house and ready for pick-up.

"And Doreen," I add. She accepted the invitation to honour her father and mother. "Maybe some others. We haven't heard back from everyone."

Who at the Becker premiere will start hissing about the signs first? Will they point and jab? Knock pews over?

I slink back from the edge of the loft. I'll disappear out the back door when the show begins. It worked for the Von Trapp Family Singers. Only Dad will come searching and drag me home. Force me to stare at loftier sights for the rest of my days— a painted-over *Creation of Adam*, lurking in the ceiling.

The first dreaded rapping comes. I return to the edge of the loft as Dad leaps out from behind the film projector cart and jogs to the door. "Come in!" he calls.

I watch Mom scamper into the kitchen to stow her dust rag below the sink.

Dad opens the door to a man with heavy glasses and a dog-eared notebook in his hand. "Is this where Martha Becker lives?"

I crouch down so only my eyes peek over the balcony edge.

"It is." Dad looks momentarily confused. "And the home of the Becker Institute! I'm so glad you've come for the screening. You're our first guest!" he adds, as though the man won a prize. "Sit wherever you like."

"I'm from the *Thorndale Sun*," the man says, twiddling his pen. I look down on the shining dome of his head, wisped with blond hair. This reporter isn't nearly as cute as the one Leanne described, but there's no time to grieve that one. I'm being hunted.

"Wonderful!" Dad says. "Take the front row."

The man interjects, but another knock interrupts him.

"John," Dad says. "Welcome!"

With heavy legs, I move to the top of the stairs and prepare to face them all.

"I'll load up the scaffolding in the truck," John says. I sink downstairs toward my imminent demise.

"Do it later, John," Dad says. "We're just about to begin the film."

I reach ground level. The reporter sits down in the front pew.

"Hello, Martha." John sends me a look as old as grade three, when the kid in the next row knows you're about to get nailed by the teacher.

"You're Martha?" The man with the notebook twists around. His eyes sweep down to my ankle socks and then up again.

I sit down in a pew. Keep to the far edge so I can see everyone's faces. "I am," I say quietly, and wonder what it's like to count down for your execution.

The door swings open. "Sorry, I'm late," Doreen says, adjusting her prayer cap. Her eyes hover just over my head. Mennonite shunning. The reporter's eyes swell at the sight of my nineteenth-century-style sister, and he scribbles in his notebook.

"This is so exciting!" Debbie's voice bubbles up from the driveway. She bustles inside. Her lips are lined in orange, a little beyond their usual borders, and a fringed shawl—some awkward attempt at glamour—tilts over one shoulder.

"Someone's here from the *Thorndale Sun*, Debbie," Dad announces from the doorway. He licks his lips.

Debbie scans the near empty pews. "Where's everyone else?"

I'd rather be electrocuted than hanged. Do you get to choose? I press against the side of the pew and feel its pine back, stiff against my spine.

Another knock. Cautiously, Mom draws open the door to Norm Schellenberger. His forehead looks red and taut.

"Norm!" Dad's arms shoot up in celebration.

Norm's eyebrows clench. "Figured I'd find out what the hell's going on around here." His left eye twitches.

Dad smiles at the reporter as if to say, "Aren't we a charming bunch? So relaxed we don't fuss over pleasantries." Then he glances out the door. "Looks like that's about it. The others must've been held up. Shall we begin? Norm, why don't you sit up front, too?"

From beside the doorway, Norm crosses his arms and stares ahead. "I'm not sitting anywhere." His voice grows louder. Lower. Angrier. "I'm just here to find out why in God's name," his eye convulses and he points a sausage finger my direction, "Your daughter smeared our entire community with those *signs*." He barks the word.

John clears his throat.

Doreen sighs and sits down.

The man with the notebook turns a page.

I've heard that some people black out before they're executed. I'd be the one fully conscious as the straps cinch around my wrists and lock into place.

"What signs?" Dad says.

Chapter 20

"*WHAT SIGNS?*" Norm sputters. "Just because they're down, doesn't mean we've forgotten them."

I grope the pew ahead for the ghost of a hymnal. Anything to occupy my hands, hot with fear.

"I know those signs!" Debbie says. "Along Putnam Road. I recorded them this morning. The film is in here somewhere." Still by the door, she rifles through her enormous canvas bag, pulls out a case and holds it high. "I can show everyone."

Camera-crazy Debbie recorded my signs. I don't know whether to laugh or climb into a hole and die slowly. I just clench my toes until the tops of my feet ache.

Dad chuckles. "I'm not sure what everyone's talking about, but it can't be as exciting as tonight's premiere." He throws back his shoulders. "We're gathered together this evening for the screening of the Becker Institute's first film." He strides to the front of the room. "Let's begin, shall we?"

Solemnly, John trudges toward the light switch. "Might as well see the signs Debbie taped, Gerald."

"What's going on?" Mom murmurs. She takes a seat on the side.

"And see the look on Gerald's face," Norm grumbles.

"They're super offensive," Debbie says with a shudder. "You've got to see them, Reverend Gerald." She waltzes to the projector, slips Dad's recording out and pops in the one from her bag. I work to regulate my breathing.

Dad parks himself on a pew near Mom. "I guess this'll be like the trailer before the main feature, Peggy." He shrugs and winks at her.

If only I could be painted out of this picture, like my *Creation of Adam*.

John dims the lights.

Putnam: Where Everyone Knows Your Business appears in the apocalyptic, glowing light of Debbie's lopsided camera frame.

"Martha made that?" The cheer disappears from Dad's voice.

Mom stifles a chuckle.

Doreen makes a clucking noise.

The reporter dips his head and scribbles.

"Just wait. They get worse," Debbie says, prancing on the spot.

Free Bullshit follows.

As the projector's piercing headlight beams, Dad makes a fist. "Impossible."

"Some kind of attitude on that girl," Norm says from the back. "She's been growing cukes on our property for I don't know how long, and now this."

Superiority Farms, Where We Think We're Better than You flickers into focus in front of Doreen's house. I glance over as she lifts her chin and turns her head from the screen.

"Oh, dear," Mom says. She clears her throat.

Lonely Acres appears and *Love Shack. No Nubs and Crooks Allowed* and all their other beastly, rectangular brethren. I bite the inside of my cheek. Debbie's camera view swings upside down, across her windshield and into darkness, probably on the way to Bernie's farm.

The screen brightens as Debbie's camerawork zooms into *But She Likes Them Beefy*.

Dad folds his arms tight at his chest. "These can't be your doing, Martha."

"The thanks we get for providing three-quarters of an acre," Norm says. "A kick in the ass is what that is."

"I'm sure my daughter didn't paint this cruel and scathing commentary," Dad says, but he doesn't sound so sure. "She only portrays uplifting subject matter."

"I wouldn't have thought she painted them either," Debbie says. "But I just noticed something. Look." She hikes up her shawl, scampers to the screen and points to the upper corner. "There's a picture of scrambled eggs snuck into the Beefy sign. Don't they look like that drawing of Martha's?"

"Seems to be the word on the street," the reporter adds. The pew creaks as he writes.

Then the final sign, *False Hopes, Turn Right*, looms before the shadowy image of our church-house, AKA the Becker Institute of Success and Higher Consciousness.

In dumbfounded silence, Dad stares ahead. I squint through the dim light. Sure enough, Mom's eyes are lingering with amusement on the sign. The reporter's pen is on pause. Doreen is peering at the mini crucifix on the wall, as though she and Jesus are sharing a quiet moment of reflection—probably a prayer for all the idiots and backstabbers in the world. I glance back at Norm. He looks ready to boil, but nothing like Dad, whose ticker seems set for an explosion that could blow everyone to smithereens.

I inhale and stand up. Grip the back of the pew ahead for steadiness. As bold and clear as I can, I announce, "I painted those signs."

Dad stares at me. "You blasted the land outside the Becker Institute with *negativity*?" A vein throbs in his neck. I never knew he had that vein.

I nod.

Dad's mouth draws a hard line. "With messages of scorn? Derision?"

I jerk at each of Dad's accusations. I ache to race out the door and into the night, away from Dad and family and Putnam. I feel like that betraying badass in the shadows of the *Last Supper.* Judas, the guy everyone still hates a bunch of centuries later. Only my likeness to Judas ends there, because Dad ain't no Jesus, and we're not in Jerusalem. We're just in Putnam, where too many eyes are looking at me for some kind of explanation.

I focus on a spot in the distance, on a knot of wood in the middle of my choir loft railing. "I needed to paint my side of the story. I'm not Miss Sunshine. I don't even like sunshine. It makes me hot and sweaty. I can't be positive and cheerful all the time. Life isn't like that."

I glance back at Dad. Surprisingly, his eyebrows have perked up. He stands, turns to face the audience and sucks in a deep breath. "Martha's messages illustrate the negativity we all strive to overcome. Haven't we all fought those annoying messages that impede our passage to personal success?"

I could swear a little lightbulb illuminates over Dad's brain just then.

"In fact," he continues, "I'll bet Martha painted those signs just for the Becker Institute's video!" He shakes his head in amazement. "And what perfect images they are."

Unbelievable. I hold my legs straight so they don't buckle under from dumb shock.

"I'm looking forward to more of Martha's paintings," he carries on, "where she shows how destructive thoughts give way to positive messages of success!" Dad's smile blazes an invitation for everyone to c'mon along with his crazy, but not quiet impossible, explanation.

A big shot Toronto lawyer couldn't have dug me out of a hole this quick.

The reporter tilts his head to one side, clicks the tail end of his pen and holds it over his notebook. Doreen's hands are clasped in prayer. John catches my eye and nods. *Take the exit*, he seems to be saying. Agreeing with Dad could solve all my problems. I'd just have to shrug innocently, paste on a cockeyed grin and the whole sign painting fiasco would be over. I glance to Mom, but she looks to the floor. I'm on my own.

I don't shrug or smile. I'm not sure whether the Becker Institute's spirit of success launches a trip through my veins, or the power of God under our pink ceiling drifts down to meet me. Or whether it's just John hurrying me along with his foot tapping the pine floor. He needs to load up his scaffolding, and I've already caused that boy enough annoyance.

I move out from the pew, walk to the front of the room and stand beside the projector. "I didn't paint signs for the Becker Institute video."

I go quiet a second, to pull my thoughts together.

I hear John cough.

"The signs are for me. And I plan to paint more. Lots more." Saying that part surprises even me. "The paintings along Putnam Road do show negativity." I glance in Norm's direction. "Cheap insults." I find Doreen's eyes. "Frustration." I look at John. "Sometimes they show a person's fears."

"The comments aren't pretty," I add, "but I was so desperate to shout them out that I didn't think how they'd affect people. And for that, I'm sorry."

I hear a low grumble from the back of the room. "Well, hallelujah."

"But I have to carry on painting," I continue. "Making honest messages, but ones that take more opinions into account than mine."

I turn off the projector. The room dims.

John gets up and flips on the lights. When he returns, he looks at me with a softness around his eyes I haven't seen for a while.

Dad opens his lips a sliver. "Well, well." He hesitates. Runs his hand along the edge of the pew. Maybe he'll exile me from the Becker Institute for Success for the rest of my life. Or maybe he won't. I eject Debbie's recording and hold its warmth against me. Either way, I'll manage. And knowing I'll manage sends me a flush of calm.

Only Dad doesn't exile me or threaten to ban paintbrushes from the house. Shining hope returns to his eyes. "I see positive outcomes in Martha's future, don't you?" he asks everyone. "What a triumph in paint! Did anyone notice her exceptional use of colour? And those varied styles of lettering? Wow!" My unstoppable, indestructible Dad grins wildly.

"Personally, I'd have chose good ol' black and white," Norm grunts from the back.

"Not for *Love Shack*," says John, running his fingers through his dark curls. "Those curvy, pink letters were just right."

"She's certainly better at graphics than Renaissance-style painting," Mom adds.

A cramp in my forehead relaxes. I can even breathe easily again. I move from the centre of the floor. I don't belong there. I'm more a behind-the-scenes kind of girl. Not like Dad. He loves centre stage. "Isn't it about time for the feature presentation?" I ask.

"You guys are going to love it," Debbie chirps from behind the projector.

Dad slides in his recording.

I turn and glance in Doreen's direction. My sister is too busy retying the bow on her prayer cap to look at me. I'm not sure I'll ever see eye to eye with a Mennonite-by-choice, but Mom settles back against her pew, looks at me and smiles.

WE DON'T CLEAN THE POPCORN off the floor until the next morning. Mom made a big bowl partway through the show. I thought Dad and Debbie did a pretty good job, for a positive thinking program. Doreen didn't pay much attention. Norm coughed and grumbled a lot. Mom and John just seemed to wait for the ending and when that happened, Debbie's applause drowned out everyone's polite clapping. But afterward, the reporter pulled Dad aside and told him the newspaper staff suffers from bouts of negativity. Dad knew just what the man was talking about and suggested a seminar. Looks like Dad has one booked for next month.

Mom sits at the communion table, drinks tea and watches me sweep kernels from under the pews.

Dad, tired out for once, is sprawled on a chair and staring at the pink ceiling. "You know what I've been thinking?" So maybe his body is tired, but his mind is still churning.

"What's that, Gerald?" Mom pulls her teabag out of her cup and rests it in her saucer.

"I was thinking about a Becker Institute televised weekly series." Dad traces the edge of an imaginary TV in the air.

"Sure, Gerald." Mom sips. "Martha, sweep up those kernels under the table too."

"*Sure, Gerald?* Well!" Dad sits taller. "That video really affected you, Peggy. Wonderful! We just need to hire a producer, secure a more professional set and design a company logo. Maybe Martha—" He stops himself.

I dump popcorn remains in the garbage.

"Or not," he says. "Martha will be busy with her own artwork."

Actually, I sketched a few rough ideas for signs on a napkin just this morning.

"She probably will." Mom wraps her hands around her teacup. "But I wish you all the best for your TV series."

"What's that supposed to mean?" Dad chuckles awkwardly. "Sounds like you're sailing me out to sea!"

I hold the broom still.

"Not really." Mom picks at a tiny blue flower on her cup. "But I won't be financing the series."

"But the Becker Institute deserves every opportunity, Peggy. We're so close to success I can taste it!" He rubs his hands together.

"Like your success at the church?" Mom's eyebrows go up, as though she's trying to question him innocently, but can't quite pull it off.

"What are you talking about?" I ask.

"Nothing important." Dad cracks his knuckles.

"You were too young to remember when Dad was a minister, Martha," says Mom.

"No need to dig up old bones!" Dad says.

"Martha should know what happened," Mom says.

"What did happen?" I ask.

"Nothing worth broadcasting," Dad says. Then he glances at the ceiling. "Although, maybe it'd be a good idea to discuss a family trait involving impulsive decisions."

"Not that the information needs to land on a hand-painted sign." Mom gives me a look. "But you should know the truth."

"No family history on signs," I agree. I'd never stab someone in the back with a paintbrush. Anymore.

"Just tell her," says Dad.

"When Dad was working at the church," Mom begins, "he had trouble with some of the Sunday School teachers."

"They had no pizzazz," Dad says. "No punch. No life."

"So he sent the teachers to a three-day inspirational workshop. All expenses paid, in Palm Springs, California." Mom downs the last of her tea. "Two thousand miles away."

Dad crosses his arms. "Those teachers needed a boost."

"I hated Sunday school," I say.

"The staff really meshed after that trip," Dad says. His eyes go dreamy.

"I bet they got good tans," I add.

"Very good," says Mom. "The trip was a great success, except for the price tag. It nearly cost the church their building. Council couldn't always afford Dad's projects. Neither can I." She stands up and pats Dad's knee. "But I'm sure you'll find success, Gerald. You're showing all the signs."

Dad and I watch as Mom carries her empty cup to the kitchen.

"The television series was just an idea." Dad shrugs.

"It's a great idea." I keep sweeping. "I bet someday you'll go for it."

Sometimes people just need a little encouragement.

Chapter 21

AS BERNIE AND I carry folded-up burlap bags to the barn, our footsteps crunch on the gravel. Cucumber season ended yesterday, when Lowe's grading station closed its doors for the season.

"Tell you what." I stop at the barn door. "Any cukes left in the field are yours." Since I kind of buggered off on picking responsibilities for the last week or three, it's the least I can offer.

"Thanks," says Bernie. "I might set up a vegetable stand and sell the leftovers." She floats a look to the distant cornfield, goes quiet and then elbows me near the ribcage. "No sign required. I'll make one myself."

"You'll sell lots of cukes by the road." I slide the barn door along its runners.

"Oh I won't set up shop there. It's too close to home."

"Then where?"

Bernie shifts her eyes like she has to think about where, only I get the funny idea she already knows.

"It's just a cucumber stand, Bern. What's the big secret? I won't commit a word to paint. Promise. Client approved messages only. Well, client considered."

Bernie sidles through the barn door and flops down her armful of bags. A plume of dust and a sweet earthy scent billow up. "I might sell cukes at the French fry truck."

"Donny Post's?" Weird.

She turns for the door. She doesn't say boo, like her mouth got glued shut.

"Why would you want to break into his territory?" I follow her out of the barn.

Bernie doesn't answer.

"Cucumbers at a French fry truck?" I muse, and realize she's leading me to my bike. "A healthy alternative?"

Bernie starts glimmering around the corners of her mouth. "Guess you could say that."

"Hey. Could you fry cukes like potatoes? French fried cucumbers?" I flip up the kickstand on my bike.

Bernie shakes her head, but her smile keeps on shining. "Doesn't work."

I settle onto the seat and stare at her. "How would you know?" Bernie isn't telling me something. Something big.

"We tried already."

"Seriously? Experimental deep-frying?" Highly weird. Especially from someone as imaginatively-challenged as Bernie. "And what do you mean 'we?'" My eyebrows feel knitted up. Then the truth hits me. "You mean you and Donny are working together?"

Her smile is fierce enough to put sunshine to shame.

"You and Donny are hanging out?"

Laughter rushes out of Bernie like a garden hose suddenly turned on full blast. "More than hanging out." She turns to face the cucumber field. "I'd say that it's over for you, me and Lowe's Pickles." She doesn't sound sad at all.

Whoa. Bernie and Donny Post. "But Bernie, Donny Post is all ... *bones.*"

She shrugs. "Sometimes what you hope for works out different in real life."

"True." I try and picture Bernie's brick-shaped self and Donny's gangly one, but even my imagination isn't that flexible. "Guess my beefy sign..."

"Sounded like you were making fun of Donny's physique? Nah. The sign made for a starting point when we had to tell Dad. He was mad at first, with Donny being older and everything, but he's coming around."

A fuzzy picture flashes in my mind of Bern and Donny's faces sticking out the window of the French fry truck, with his face cranked over top and hers shining below. I suppose I could tweak that picture into focus. "Do Leanne and Tammy know?"

"Not yet. Doesn't matter either way. Listen, I'm heading over to Donny's now." She takes a few steps backwards.

"Wait." I grab the sleeve of her T-shirt. I can't let Bernie waltz off the farm this quick, not without telling me more. "How long have you two been... "

"Friendly?"

I scratch the side of my neck and think of Donny's stooped frame. "Yeah."

Bernie peers up at an invisible calendar in the sky. Her feet are already pointing in a different direction from me. "A couple of months."

All season long and she didn't say a word. Or maybe she did and I wasn't paying attention.

"Did I tell you we're thinking of moving to P.E.I.?" she adds. "Potato country."

My jaw goes slack. "You didn't."

"Not today or anything." Bernie speeds up her words like she wants to cut short our chat. "Come by the truck sometime. I'll cut you a deal on late season cukes. No nubs or crooks. Premium grade only," she calls back, already sashaying down the gravel lane.

I stand on my pedals and start toward home. For the first mile, I push down a droopy feeling. Prince Edward Island seems so far away. But by the time I reach Putnam, the droopiness gives way to something more uplifting, and as I crest the hill toward our church-house, a sign takes shape in my mind.

A FEW WEEKS LATER, I'm surrounded by goopy paint tins on the patch of grass behind Donny Post's French fry truck. Donny always takes Sundays off. Bernie, too, so I'm safe to paint without detection.

I turn the blue plastic milk crate upside down and sit. I still haven't heard from Velvet. I doubt I ever will, although I did see an article in the *Toronto Star* a few days ago, near the bottom of a page. It was about a recent show of sign paintings at a small gallery. Even before I read the article, I'd already convinced myself that my collection of signs wouldn't be hitting the National Gallery any time soon. The article confirmed my suspicions. It said the works seemed out of context in a gallery setting, and in need of development in both concept and technique. I guess Velvet will have to find honesty in art in her own time, however long that takes.

The *Thorndale Sun* reporter who came to the screening was kinder. He said my signs were intriguing and daring, not that I have anything to show for them. I'll use my newer pieces of sign-art when I apply to colleges next year.

A car engine's whine dwindles behind me and cuts. I peek around the edge of the truck.

"Leanne made us late," Tammy Mills calls out the car window. "Had to do her hair." They climb out, and with similarly coiffed heads, bob toward me.

"Find a paintbrush. I brought lots." I lead them around to the back of Donny's truck and nod to the plastic bag on the grass.

"This better be the kind of paint that washes out of your clothes," Leanne says.

I dip my brush into a paint tin, load her up good and hurl a gob of green toward Leanne's shirt. Bull's eye. "Give it a wash and let me know."

"Thanks a lot." Paint oozes down Leanne's shirt.

Tammy Mills hoots.

"Lots of colours to choose from over here," I add.

Leanne holds her shirt off her front and bends down to survey the choices on the grass. "Pumpkin Orange." She whistles, lets go her sopping shirt and pries off the lid. "Turn around, Martha. This one's for you."

I walk over, turn and lean forward.

"You're letting her?" Tammy Mills says.

"Why not?"

"Hold onto the hem." Leanne pulls brushstrokes over the back of my shirt. "The material keeps bunching up."

Cool moisture soaks through the fabric. Leanne steps back.

"*Paint Bitch,*" Tammy Mills reads slowly.

"Perfect," I say. "Let's get started."

"We'll have to hurry," Leanne says. "Donny and Bern leave tomorrow."

"Why would anyone want to move to P.E.I?" Tammy Mills asks.

"They're in love," Leanne answers. "Doesn't matter where they are."

"Maybe she needs space from Norm," I say. I'll miss ol' Bern. She promised to call as soon as they arrive, but still. "Or maybe she needs a break from pressures to buy vodka for under-agers."

"No," Leanne says. "She'll miss feeling needed. I'm giving her a brand new bottle as a memory of us."

"You're giving away alcohol?" I ask.

"You don't think I'm capable of generosity with beverages?"

"Leanne's fake ID is working out real good," Tammy Mills says.

Leanne returns the lid to the orange tin and smiles.

"All right listen," I say. "I painted the heart already." I squat next to the truck and point out the lopsided shape above the license plate. "And I penciled in *Just Married, Sort Of.* One of you can blotch flowers around the heart, like the ones people make from Kleenex. Tammy Mills could do that."

"I love those flowers," says Tammy Mills.

"Martha," Leanne says, staring at the side of my head. "Did you get your ears pierced?"

"I guess I did."

"What in hell kind of earring is that?"

Like a New York runway model, I fling back my hair to expose my earlobe, ornamented with a small hoop that circles a diamond ring. "It's Doreen's engagement ring."

"I thought you swallowed it," Leanne says. Tammy Mills leans in for inspection.

"My mom found it when she was scraping dishes after Anna's birthday. John stuck the ring in his own piece of cake by accident." After Mom found the ring, she hid it. She wasn't so sure about John and me getting married, but after seeing my signs, she figured I can work that one out on my own.

"Then what happened to the rest of the wedding rings?" Tammy Mills asks.

"I can't say right now." I shuffle the paintbrushes around.

"Sure you can," Leanne says.

"Nope. It's private."

I gave Bernie and Donny the rings. They're considering a garden wedding in a few years, after Bernie finishes her college program in Charlottetown.

"I can't believe you're finally pierced," Tammy Mills says, still gawking at my ear.

"Martha's a late bloomer," Leanne says. "Too bad about the rest of her development." She waves her brush toward my chest.

"At least I don't have a fat ass."

"I do," Tammy Mills says.

"Let's paint it," Leanne suggests. "We can stamp your butt on the trailer for your signature."

"Good idea," I say.

"All right," Tammy Mills says.

"I could stamp my ample bosom," Leanne says. "My shirt's wrecked anyway."

"I'll leave my company info near the bumper." *Martha's Rebel Signage. Raw messages. Gutsy designs.* It's on my sign, too. The new one I hammered close to the road in front of John's shed, where light streams through the cracks in his ceiling and the birds perch in the rafters. I'm storing my paint tins in Doreen's old oak dresser. John is going easy on the rent, but it's purely professional between us. Personally, I'm not that into guys with navy coveralls and John Deere caps, although John says guys like him can wear a girl down until she's utterly helpless to their otherworldly powers.

I'm not so sure about that, but you never know.

Leanne and Tammy dip brushes into their paint cans. As they start in on the Kleenex flowerlike designs, I swing my plastic milk crate around and sit down before the next string of letters.